THE FLOWERS AT FLOOD HOUSE

THE FLOWERS AT FLOOD HOUSE

J.J. WALKER

THE FLOWERS AT FLOOD HOUSE

Cover art: Matt Seff Barnes Art

Editor: Shawna Hampton

Interior design: J.J. Walker

jjwalkerwrites.com

Paperback ISBN: 978-1-7389906-4-1

Ebook ISBN: 978-1-7389906-5-8

For Nan P.

AUTHOR'S NOTE

On December 29th, 2023, I lost my grandmother to dementia. I remember my dad saying it was like he'd been living with a stranger who was possessed, desperate for an exorcism. The experience was grueling, unforgiving, and one I won't forget.

I started writing this story at the start of the steep decline that would eventually end her struggle. I think it was my way of coping. An attempt to figure out what we were dealing with.

While *The Flowers at Flood House* didn't end up being a direct exploration of dementia or any other neurodegenerative disease, it did end up being a story about memories. How they shape us. How they haunt us. How painful the ache can be with and without them.

1

Gina Carter got the call after midnight. The room had been dark and too warm for spring. It had taken her a moment to push away the thickness of sleep and absorb what the person at the end of the line was saying.

"Did you hear me? She's naked," the voice said. "Not a single piece of clothing on her body."

"Who is?"

"I told you, I don't know. But she's old. I would have stayed—really, I would—but I was creeped out."

"Alright, alright. Where did you see her?"

"Salem Road. You should send someone out there. Check she's alright."

It would have been easier to do that. Delegate the dilemma and make it someone else's problem, but Stillwater's well-being was more than a job. For Gina, it was a way of life.

She pulled herself out of bed, put on her boots and jacket, ran some gel through her short peroxide-blond hair, and checked her pockets for her police badge. She'd called her partner, Trey—dragged his sorry ass out of bed—and together they'd driven out to Salem Road in her squad car with lights so bright they cut the Stillwater night like butter.

As they approached the deep curve where Salem Road started, Gina moved her hand to her pistol, reassuring herself with its firmness. Stillwater wasn't familiar with violence, but that wasn't to say something couldn't happen. Whether they were dealing with an old woman or not, there were a lot of trees out here. A lot of places to hide.

"He said she was naked," Gina announced.

"You already told me," Trey said, shifting in his seat. He yawned, using the mirror to flatten hair poking at an odd angle where it had been resting on the pillow. "Who called you anyway?"

"Martin," Gina said, slowing the car to a crawl. She squinted, looking left and right into the thick forest that surrounded them.

"Cline? Now I know why no one stuck around. Guy's a pussy."

"Yeah." Gina sighed. "One of the problems working a town this small. Everyone's got a direct line to a cop."

As the car edged up Salem Road, the trees didn't give up their thickness. For many, that thickness was part of Stillwater's charm. Visitors found serenity in the green. Escape in all the leaves. It was the reason it topped internet lists promising relief from the city.

"There." Trey pointed, but Gina wouldn't have missed her. Everything Martin Cline had said was true. She was alone. Old. Standing in the middle of the road without a single piece of clothing on her body.

"I know who that is," Gina murmured.

The old woman turned to stare at them as Gina lifted herself out of the car. The little gray hair she had caught in the headlight's glare like candy floss, and parts of her skin sagged so much the light struggled to fill its wrinkles.

"Get your hand off your gun, for Christ's sake," Gina snapped over the car's roof. "And find something to cover her up."

Gina put her hands out as she closed the distance. She was only a few steps away when she saw the smile die on the old woman's lips, and the curl of her mouth replace the happiness with concern.

"It's Marsha, right?" Gina said. "Marsha Dorsey?"

"Have you seen my husband?"

"Your husband?"

"Yes, my husband. Sully. We were skinny-dipping and... and he always does this. Takes my clothes. Runs off with them. It's this game he likes to play."

Everyone in Stillwater had heard about the woman in front of Gina. She'd moved into Flood House with her son, Seth, occupying a house that had stood empty and neglected for years. Seth had bought the place because her mind was sick, and he wanted somewhere quiet where she could get better. Only, there was never mention of a husband. As far as Gina, and the rest of Stillwater was concerned, he was dead or didn't exist.

"Marsha, I don't know where your husband is, but let's get you covered up." She grabbed the blanket from Trey, wrapping it around shoulders so skinny, the bones felt sharp.

"But he was here. We were just swimming in the sea."

"I know, Marsha." Gina shot Trey a knowing look, shaking her head to stop whatever he was about to say from leaving his mouth. "Let's get you in the car. Take you home."

Marsha pushed away from Gina with such force, Gina wondered where the strength had come from.

"I'm not leaving without my husband."

"Marsha."

"I'm not leaving! You come near me and I'll pull your eyes out."

"Jesus," Trey muttered.

"Your husband is at home," Gina lied. "Alright? Come with us to the car and we'll take you to him. There's nothing for you to worry about." She watched Marsha process the words. Watched as the eyebrows creased and the eyes glazed with a dull and lifeless vacancy.

"He's at home?"

"Yes, Marsha. He's at home. We'll take you to him. How does that sound?"

Marsha nodded. Gina took her hand, flinching at how cold it felt. Nobody said another word until Marsha was sitting in the back of the car under a blanket that swallowed her body.

"This ain't right," Trey whispered as he snapped the belt into its buckle. "Someone like that needs to be in a home. A place with proper care. Not in that old house with a son who doesn't even know when she's missing."

"You're telling me," Gina replied, keeping her voice low, looking over her shoulder to offer Marsha a warm smile.

They stayed quiet as they swept across Stillwater. Marsha made no sound until they turned into the tunnel of leaves that separated Flood House from the small town. At first she shifted in her seat. Then it was movements of panic: twitches, fidgets, pulling at her seat belt.

"No," she whispered. "No, no, no."

"It's ok, Marsha," Trey said, turning. "We're taking you home. We're almost there."

"No! This isn't my home. This isn't my house."

"This *is* your home, Marsha," Gina started. "You moved here with Seth. Your son, Seth. Do you remember?"

"I don't care," Marsha shouted, removing her belt. "I'm not going back in there." The buckle made a hollow *ting* as it hit off the glass. She pulled hard at the door's handle.

"Marsha, stop. It's ok. Try and breathe for me."

"No."

"Marsha."

"No! Please don't make me go in there. I don't want to go back in there. Not with those flowers. Not with that man. Not in that house!"

2

FOUR MONTHS LATER

Seth was perched on the edge of his bed, rubbing thumb and forefinger into tired eyes, when he heard it.

Since moving to Stillwater with his mother, he'd become familiar with her voice. The way it sounded thrown to the top of Flood House, asking where he was or why it was so cold. Only, that summer was anything but cold, and that shout had been a scream.

"Mom?" He lifted his head for an answer, eyes heavy with restless sleep. The vest he was wearing clung to a protruding belly, a dark stain defining its front. "Mom! Son of a bitch," he said, grunting as he pushed his body off a pile of sheets knotted together with sweat.

He moved his feet into the holes he'd left when he stepped out of his jeans the night before, pulled the jeans up, tightened the belt around his belly, and left the room for stairs that complained against his weight.

"Mom. Answer me."

As he reached their bottom, he saw Marsha standing at the end of the hallway, looking into the house's basement. She was dressed in tracksuit pants and a faded T-shirt, holding a cup still waiting for coffee. When he reached her and took a few steps through the door's tired frame, he saw what was waiting down there, and what had gotten his mother so rattled.

The ceiling was thick with them, its wooden beams smothered in bunches of dried flowers hanging upside down. Daisies sat next to daffodils. Roses were paired with rhododendrons. Seth saw that each bunch was held together with string, attached to the room's exposed wood with what looked like nails. Their petals were brittle. Their stems were sharp, overlapping in kaleidoscopic pockets of color.

If it wasn't for the shock of it, the realization that someone had been in his house, he might have been impressed. He may have even said it was beautiful.

"Mom, get away from the basement."

"But..."

"Mom!" Seth put a hand on her arm, leading her away from the stairs. "Get away from the *damned* basement."

She followed his lead, retreating into the kitchen, where she stood next to a table topped with dirty plates from last night's dinner.

"Where are you going? Seth!"

Seth panted as he pulled himself up the stairs. When he returned with the shotgun he'd been sleeping next to, he saw disappointment line her face, and she made her hatred known with a loud tut. Ignoring her, he unlatched the kitchen door and stepped onto the back porch. The humidity swelled so fast around him that he felt sweat pressing out of his pores. As he stepped off the rotted wood onto solid ground, away from Flood House, unkempt grass tickled his ankles.

He swept the gun across the land at the back of the house. At the other end of a yard that needed cutting, trees grew so thick they formed a wall, their branches long and drooping as though they were filled with sadness. Behind him, Flood House's old and weathered walls watched, its porch a different color from what it had been yesterday.

He couldn't check every trunk or tree—there were too many of them—but when he was satisfied no one was hiding in plain sight, he lowered the weapon, hand up to shield his eyes from the morning sun.

He made his way back into the kitchen. The smell of unwashed plates clung to him as he moved past Marsha to the top of the basement stairs.

He entered slowly. The stair treads groaned until he felt his feet meet the basement's cold, hard ground. Under the light of a single exposed bulb sat the house's organs. Old pipes and exposed wires. Boxes he still had to unpack. He reached up. Went to press a bunch of the flowers between thumb and forefinger, but pulled away at the last moment, worried they'd be filled with poison and he'd feel his skin burn. He found comfort in the grip of his shotgun, wondering if someone in Stillwater would take a joke that far.

"So many flowers."

"Get upstairs," Seth said over his shoulder. "Go on. Finish making your coffee. I'll take one too."

"And they're all dried out," his mother continued, ignoring him. "Would've taken someone a long time to do something like that. To hang them all up like that."

"Go on," Seth said, irritation firming his voice. "Get your ass upstairs."

He watched his mother shake her head. Watched until her thin frame had disappeared and he heard the sound of the kitchen door closing behind her.

He did an entire rotation of the basement, wheezing as he bent his legs to look under an old shelving unit, around the house's waste pipe, and between two boxes of tax returns and bank statements that needed filing.

Aside from the flowers, the basement remained as he'd left it. Not knowing what he could or should do down there, he left, groaning as he went back upstairs.

When he reentered the kitchen, he was glad to see his mother with her head in the fridge, muttering something to herself. They say the devil makes work for idle thumbs, and for Marsha Dorsey, caught in a disease slowly eating at her mind, that couldn't be truer.

"I told you there were flowers down there," she said, struggling to lift a heavy slice of watermelon out of the fridge. "And you didn't believe me."

"Not now, Mom."

"What're you doing?"

"Making a call."

"To who?"

"Yanna."

Marsha let out a sarcastic laugh, throwing her head back for dramatic effect. "And just what is she gonna do?"

"Mom, I said not now," Seth grumbled, phone already trapped between ear and shoulder, the cord running ringlets down the front of his shirt. "Yanna. Yeah, it's me. Can you come down here? Soon as you can. Yes, yes, she's fine." He chanced a look at Marsha, who was dribbling watermelon juice down her front. "Not this time. It's something else. Something different. Alright. Yeah. We'll see you."

Seth put the phone down, dropping the shotgun from his shoulder into a cupped hand.

"Now where are you going?" Marsha yelled.

"Outside."

"Why?"

"To wait," Seth shouted behind him.

"To wait." He heard his mother release another dry laugh. "Months you've been waiting on that woman. I say it's time you set your cards on the table. Say how you feel so she can reject you and put us all out of our damn misery."

3

YANNA'S CAR pulled into the drive just after ten. Even without seeing it amble down the dirt track, out of the tunnel of twisted leaves and overgrowth that stretched away from Flood House, Seth would have recognized the sound of that tired engine. It stopped and he pushed himself off a seat that rocked on the front porch after him. As he threw what remained of his coffee on the dry earth, he tried to ignore how fresh the paint looked around the front door they'd never used.

"What took you so long?"

"Oh, quit your moaning," Yanna shouted out of the car's open window. "I'm here now, ain't I?" She killed the engine, using the open window to pull herself out of the vehicle. She was wearing jeans and a plaid shirt, her bright red hair hanging around a freckled face and a button nose warm with sunburn. "So? What is it?"

"There's something you've got to see."

"Your mom?"

"Mom's fine," Seth said. "It's something else."

"Well, stop messing around, will you? My shift starts in

an hour, and after everything that's been happening here, you're making me worried."

Seth didn't say anything. Instead, he turned, prompting her to follow him around the side of the house.

"Where is she?"

"Napping," Seth said as he led Yanna through the kitchen. "I'm not complaining. I'll take any quiet I can get." He rounded the hallway to the top of the basement stairs, switched on the light, and led her into its depths.

When he saw the space was empty, full of nothing but old pipes and boxes, all its flowers gone, his blood ran cold. As he stared at the same view he'd seen every time he went down there, filled with the usual dust and dead air, he wondered whether it was what he'd been wishing for, or if he'd just discovered that he, like his mother, was losing his mind.

"I don't understand," Seth said. "They...they were here."

"What were?"

"Flowers."

"Flowers?"

"Hundreds of them. All dried out. In bunches. Hanging upside down from the ceiling."

"How in God's name would something like that get there? And why would someone do something like that?" Yanna said, gaze transfixed on the emptiness in front of them.

Seth moved into the center of the room. He leaned back, examining the wooden beams stretched over their heads, checking for nail marks or dents, stray petals, or broken stalks on the floor around him.

"I don't know. Woke up and they were there."

"Here?"

"Right here. Everywhere."

Yanna joined him. She looked up, squinting at the undisturbed wood. He recalled how he'd approached the flowers earlier, avoided touching them in case they were poisonous, and felt an odd uncertainty stirring in his belly. "I think it's those Waite boys."

"The Waite boys?" Yanna was so surprised, she turned to look at him. "Seth. Think about what you're saying."

"I thought about it."

"And?"

"I think they did it."

"You're kidding?"

"I'm not. I heard what they've been saying about us. After what Marsha did to their mom, they don't like us here. They've had it in for us for weeks."

"Oh, Seth. Come on."

"I'm serious. To them this might be a prank, but this is our home. What we're talking about is vandalism. A break-in. They have no idea how much this is going to unsettle Mom."

"I know, Seth. But listen to yourself. If what you're saying is true, and you had that many flowers here, then it's something that's clearly had thought behind it. Something like that has to be considered. *Organized.*"

Seth grumbled.

"You got any idea of the work that would have to go into something like that? To collect them, dry them out, and then get them into the house and set them up, all without waking you or Marsha up? And what's the point of it? Of all the things they could bring into your house, they choose that. The Waite boys couldn't put a bunch of flowers together if their lives depended on it."

"I suppose."

"You suppose?"

"I *know*," Seth grumbled, admitting defeat.

"You can have it in for those boys as much as you want, but the only things they're good at putting together is mean words. We both know they're not smart. There's no way in hell they could've done something like that." Yanna exhaled, hand on hip. "But regardless of who did it, I'm worried about you, Seth. What with your mom and how she's been. Have you been sleeping? Eating?"

"Yeah," he said dryly, using the back of his hand to wipe sweat pooled where thick hair used to be.

"You promise?"

"I promise," he said, noting the worry on her face. "You don't believe me, do you?"

Yanna looked away, pressing the tip of her boot into the room's foundation. "Have you thought about what I said last week? What we talked about?"

"When?"

"Last Thursday. We ate your favorite—ribs and coleslaw with—"

"Triple-fried fries, yeah, yeah. You said you think I'm losing my mind. Getting things muddled. Same as Mom. That I may need some help up here. I remember."

"Seth, I didn't say you were losing your mind. I just said—"

"I'm not lying. There were flowers in this basement. Hanging. Dried out and arranged across this entire ceiling. Mom saw it too. Go and ask her." He turned away, knowing how hollow it sounded, asking someone with a failing mind to clarify whether something was real.

"Look, if you say there were flowers here, then I believe you. You have no reason to lie."

Seth let out a sarcastic laugh.

"Really, I do," Yanna said.

"But?"

"But nothing."

The silence settled again. They both looked at their feet, letting the hum of the house fill in the gaps until it lulled the conversation back on track.

"I don't know who did it," Seth began again. "I don't know how they did it. I don't know where they got them from, and I don't know how they got it all here. And I sure as hell don't know where they all went. But with a lot of work comes a lot of pride."

"Damn straight," Yanna said, offering a firm nod.

"So I struggle to believe they won't be back. That they won't try something again. I know they will. And I'll be here. Waiting."

4

It had taken over an hour to get Marsha settled into bed. The more the weeks passed, the harder it was getting. He'd tried to get a routine in place, but she was becoming aggressive, unpredictable. Sundowning, they called it. A change in behavior when the light disappears. Recently, as day turned to night, her comments had grown barbs and her criticisms cruel, thrown with no concern for where those sharp points might land.

Only two nights ago, Seth had found her in the yard, grass up to her knees, dressed in clothes he'd not seen her wearing since he was a teenager, asking where she could get the bus into town for a job interview. When he'd tried to coax her inside, she'd turned aggressive, shouting, asking why a man pretending to be a dentist was attacking her.

They'd only been in Stillwater five months, but already, those months had felt like an eternity. He was tired of thinking about whether he'd made the right decision. Tired of deliberating whether he'd done what was best for her. The house was cheap, in a quiet town with a decent reputation, and that's all he'd wanted. A place where he could focus on looking after her. A place where, maybe, she would get better.

Around him, the night was thick, its dark so inky it felt purple. With a beer in one hand, he might have mistaken it for any other evening. It had been common for Seth to spend the night under an uncovered bulb, surrounded by the buzz of insects, thinking, sipping a cold bottle until he reached its bottom. He liked the quiet of it. The drone would often send him to sleep. The only difference tonight was that he'd had dried flowers in his basement, and he was sitting with a shotgun draped across his lap.

He'd considered calling the cops. Considered asking Yanna's sister, Gina, to drop by and offer her verdict, but thought better of it. Not after her and Trey had found Marsha naked out on Salem Road and brought her back kicking and screaming, with a few harsh words gripped between their teeth. Not after the incident at Ed's grocery store a few months ago, when Marsha had tried to push her fingers into Kathy Waite's eyes, fearing they were evil and "needed to be popped."

Marsha's fingers had still been warm from the edges of Kathy's eye sockets when Gina had reappeared at Flood House. Instead of being forgiving, and understanding, she'd told him Stillwater was a quiet community that didn't need that kind of disruption. "Your mom's upsetting a lot of people," she'd said. "Perhaps it's time you reassess her situation."

From that moment, he'd felt like a burden in a place that should have been home. He shopped for groceries in the moments it was quietest. Took Marsha for walks along the main streets in the morning, when the sun was just appearing. In a handful of months, they'd turned from objects of curiosity to threats.

No. If the creator of this elaborate prank showed up, Seth wanted to be able to speak with them openly, without anybody looking over his shoulder.

He thought back to what Yanna had said to him. Yanna, the only person who, for whatever reason, had continued giving them a chance. The only person willing to show empathy and compassion after everything that had happened. She didn't seem to care that Marsha was found naked on Salem Road or that she'd almost taken someone's eyes out. All she cared about was offering them company. Even with the disbelief on her face today, her company was enough.

The house's lights pooled before him. His mind went back to the flowers. They'd been there. He'd reached out to their cold petals and seen the vibrancy in their colors. His mother's memory might be failing, but his wasn't. His was still sharp.

He took another sip of beer. A light breeze dried sweat against his face. From somewhere out in the dark, a noise reached him. At first, he wondered whether it was an animal—an elk, or some sort of bird.

But when he attached himself to the idea that the sound was feet moving through long grass, he put his drink on the porch and gripped the shotgun in both hands. He pointed its barrel out into the black. He heard a rustle again: the sound of grass on fabric.

"Who's there?"

The noise stopped. When no one answered, he gripped the gun tighter, standing up, bringing the butt into his shoulder's thick flesh.

"Get out here," Seth said. "I knew you'd be too proud to let a thing like that go. You wanted the satisfaction of seeing what I thought of it, didn't you? If you're one of those Waite boys, I swear to God."

Seth leaned forward, squinting, aware of a thicker mass in all that black.

He heard something behind him. A voice in the house. He swung the shotgun around to meet it, a damp unease licking at his back.

He was sure it had been a voice. A woman's. Crying out somewhere in one of the rooms.

"Mom?" Seth tried to shout, but fear made his voice tremble. "Mom!"

With one hand on the gun, finger pressed against the trigger, he used the other to open the kitchen door. He stepped into Flood House, closed and locked the door behind him.

He held his breath. He wanted to hear how the house moved. Wanted to hear if it was supporting more weight than it should.

All was quiet.

Silent, until it wasn't.

A scream tore itself through the house. There was a bang in the basement. The sound of something hitting hard floor.

"Mom!" Seth moved. Lunged from the kitchen into Flood House's corridors, open like a vein carrying him to the problem's heart. He rounded the corner, down the stairs into the basement, and saw her lying on the floor. Her nightgown was wrapped around her frail figure, making her look like a long, thin sack of potatoes.

"No, no, no, no, no."

Seth put the gun down. Fell to her. "Mom," he moaned. His hands skirted the air above her. Around her. He didn't know what to touch. What to do or grab first. Eventually, he settled on her shoulders. He held them. Lifted them slightly so he could rest her head on his lap.

"Mom. Mom, talk to me! What happened?"

Even in the bad light of the room's exposed bulb, he could see everything was different. Not just different, but wrong. Her skin. Its color. The way her eyes moved around her skull. He checked her breathing. Felt the irregular beating of her heart. He didn't know what had happened or how she'd gotten there. Didn't know whether to comfort her or call for help.

What he did know was that he was losing her. With every second that passed, her life was slipping from his grip, and he came closer to the overwhelming realization that she might be dying.

Another sound echoed from upstairs. Footsteps on floorboards. The sound of someone walking around.

Seth thought about looking for their source. Thought about searching the house for it and using his shotgun to blow a big hole in its belly, but he didn't want to leave her.

Not as Marsha was breathing her last breaths. Not as the light was leaving his mother's eyes.

5

Before John Carter placed the plastic divider on the checkout's conveyor, Yanna knew what he'd be buying. Milk, bread, eggs, and a packet of processed ham. If he was feeling adventurous, there'd be a banana. As he added the produce to the sticky surface, she realized adventure wasn't on the menu.

She pressed the button next to her and the counter ate the belt.

"Some sort of commotion going on out there," John said, nodding a lazy chin toward the store's entrance.

"That so?"

"Yes, ma'am. Saw your sister and Trey driving out somewhere real early this morning. Had their sirens on too."

"Yeah?" Yanna said. She looked out of the store's large windows. The early morning's sun streamed onto signs promoting fresh fruit and vegetables and two-for-one deals on pancake mix beside a pile of bright red baskets. She thought of her sister, Gina, Stillwater's highest-ranking police officer. Hoped, as she always did, that she would make it home safe. "I'm sure it's nothing," she continued, scanning the bread and milk, opening the carton of eggs to check that none had cracked.

"I wouldn't be so sure," John said. "World's crazy. Need people like your sister more than ever. I'll be honest, Yan. I'm glad I grew up when I did."

"Cash?"

"Yes, ma'am."

As the morning grew into its heat, so did an uncertainty in Yanna. John left, others arrived, and she spent the day as she usually did: scanning items, stacking shelves, and taking too many cigarette breaks. What should have been an average day was exactly that, until it wasn't.

It wasn't what she was doing that changed, but the energy of those around her. People had become alert. Charged. They looked at her differently. Approached her as if she was infected. For all the effort she put into ignoring it, it didn't take long for Yanna to come to the conclusion that Stillwater knew something she didn't.

By the time the store's owner, Edgar Britt, pulled her aside and asked if he could have a word in his office, Yanna was convinced everyone had found out she was getting fired.

As they started toward his office, down corridors bruised with years of wear and tear, she began counting how many days her money would last her, and what she could have done to lose her job. She'd only ever stolen a couple of chocolate bars. A packet of muffins. She'd arrived late, taken a lot of breaks, but Edgar was a smoker. He understood. Right?

Edgar was a skinny man with thick glasses and a voice that had never recovered its firmness after he lost his wife to cancer. Yanna had known him long enough to see him deal with the aftermath of that death. Been working at the store long enough to see them work through every round of chemo. This place had become her routine. Her DNA. Closing the office door behind her, she struggled with the idea that it was almost over, and swallowed the uncertainty lodged in her throat.

"Sit down, Yanna," Edgar said, motioning to a frayed office chair. She did, moving the stack of paper towering under a paperweight with a seashell in the middle.

"How're you doing?"

"I'm ok," Yanna said.

"How's it been today?"

"What's up, Ed? If you're getting ready to fire me, these polite questions won't mean shit."

"You seen your sister today?"

"No. I saw John, who said he saw her driving somewhere early. Mentioned there might be something happening. Why?"

Edgar nodded. Yanna could sense he was nervous. It was the biting around the bottom of his nails. If something wasn't right, he'd start chewing, peeling back a layer of skin. From where she was sat, she could see one close to bleeding.

"I just got a call from Trey. He said Gina's been trying to get a hold of you."

"I was running late this morning. Left my cell at home."

"Right."

"Will you tell me what's going on? Is she hurt?"

Edgar exhaled loudly. "It's Marsha."

"Marsha? Seth's Marsha? Marsha Dorsey? What about her?"

"She's dead, Yanna."

Yanna let out a sound between confusion and disgust, her brow creasing.

"What?"

"I'm so sorry," Edgar said, pushing himself forward. He put his hand on her arm, letting out a wheeze. She pulled away, and the chair cracked loudly behind her.

"But why? How? I was with her yesterday."

"I know you were close."

"What happened?"

"I don't know the details," he said, using his hands to calm her down. "Trey didn't tell me. But after what happened here with Kathy—what happened out on Salem Road—I can't say I'm surprised. The woman was sick, Yanna. She should have been getting proper help."

"I don't understand."

"Gina will want to talk to you. I couldn't just sit there and not tell you. Figured it was better coming from me than someone blurting it out. You know how quickly stuff gets around."

Yanna closed her eyes, mind on fire. She thought back to Seth's voice, letting its rumble take over her thoughts. She saw his smile and the concern that had lined his face the day before. Saw the worry at the thought of flowers in his basement. She couldn't believe she'd been with them hours ago. Couldn't believe Marsha was dead.

"I want you to go home. Take the rest of the day," Edgar continued. "Tomorrow too. Hell, take as long as you need."

A weakness started to infect her knees. She felt the same pressure spread to her fingers, gripped tightly around the chair's arms. She felt sick, unsettled, and wondered whether she'd ever be able to get up again.

"Where's Gina now?"

"I don't know. I imagine she's at Seth's, but I told Trey you would call her, so that's what you'll do. You'll go home, and you'll call your sister. Alright?"

Yanna nodded, and before she could register anything else, that's where she was. Home.

She didn't remember what she said to Edgar. Couldn't remember whether her legs had held her weight, or whether her fingers were hurting from how hard they'd gripped the chair or the steering wheel.

All she knew was that she was standing in her living room, looking out the window at a group of boys and girls comparing how far they could skid on bikes too big for them. Then her ear was pressed against something solid, and the ringing felt so overwhelming and sharp in her head, she had to lower its volume.

"Yanna."

"What happened?"

"Where are you?"

"Gina, what happened?"

Yanna heard the release of breath. In it, she heard how many times the lines between family and the force had been blurred. Too many times, her sister had told Yanna things she shouldn't have, readjusting the lens with which she saw people living in and around Stillwater. Drunk driving. Assault. A drug habit turned violent. Too many times, Yanna had asked questions that would get anyone else into trouble, and Gina had said she couldn't tell her, until she did.

Only this time, the details concerned her. This time, they mattered.

"We're still trying to figure out the specifics, but from what I can see, it was a heart attack."

"What?"

"A heart attack. Plain and simple."

"Plain and simple. You could at least say it with some love in your voice."

"Yanna, this is my job. It's how it works. She was an old woman who clearly had a lot of issues. It was just her time to go."

"And Seth?"

"He's fine. Processing. Figuring it out. He'll be alright."

"I was there yesterday. She was fine."

"I don't know, Yanna. It happens. There's nothing else I can say. An old woman died. We'll get the paperwork filed and get Seth the help he needs."

Yanna stayed quiet. The commotion of other voices tinged with static filled the silence. She wondered whether Gina was standing where she'd been standing the day before, when Seth's mother was alive enough to bring air into her lungs. She imagined strange shoes in Seth's house, dirtying the kitchen floor, leaving the door open for insects. She didn't like it. Didn't like any of it. Was close to screaming that they all needed to leave. Get out of their house. Let the place, and Seth, breathe. In the distance, she heard someone call Gina's name.

"Look, Yanna. I've got to go. I'll stop by tonight. Bring you some dinner. Check if you're doing ok. Yanna?"

"Yeah, yeah. Whatever," Yanna said. A swell of emotions threatened to unsteady her. Then Gina abandoned her. The line went dead, and she let the swell consume her.

6

Yanna had been leaving the swimming pool when she'd received the call. A single impact to the head. That's all it had taken to kill her and Gina's mother. Almost fifty years erased by bad footing in the shower.

While Gina had thrown herself into purpose—joining Stillwater's police force, using constant praise and affirmation to keep going—Yanna had entered a period of grief and loneliness so thick and pure she wondered whether she'd ever be able to pull herself out of its syrup.

Throughout the pain, she imagined herself in an ocean, the endless sky above, an endless black below, and all she could do with it was tread water.

While Marsha's death had disturbed the dust she'd let fall on those feelings, it made her think of Seth. What he was going through. How he was feeling. How much it all ached. Last night, Gina never followed through on her promise of dinner. Ed stopped by with a pack of beers, and her neighbor, Rose, left chicken pie on the doorstep, but she knew Seth wasn't getting the same treatment. There wouldn't be beer or food waiting on his doorstep that morning, or a familiar voice at the end of the phone. As she had done with her mother, he would be figuring this out alone.

Yanna winced as the ground made contact with the bottom of her car. It was loud, hitting the undercarriage so hard the rock music skipped. It brought her out of thoughts for Seth and Marsha to a fresh concern of whether she needed to visit the mechanic.

Ahead, the road looked the same as she'd left it: dirty, uneven, but familiar. Around her, branches sagged like backs with poor posture and the air was so humid it felt claustrophobic.

As Flood House unfurled through the thick green, she expected to see him sitting on the porch, with his unclean shirt and a beer resting on his belly, waiting with a worried look on his face. The morning he said he'd seen flowers in the basement wasn't the first time she'd pulled up to answer his concerns, but now she wondered whether she'd done so with enough warmth.

She shook the guilt away, pulling her car to a stop in her usual spot in front of Seth's rusted truck.

She cut the engine and sat a moment, taking everything in through a windscreen marred with dirt and dead bugs, thinking about what she could or should say to a man who'd just lost his mother. A man she suddenly felt she didn't know at all.

Flood House watched her. It looked worn. Well lived-in. Throughout Yanna's life, it had been known for its emptiness, but now, she saw it as a coffin. A house Marsha had spent her last breaths in.

Now, its presence stretched across the flat landscape like a giant bruise. Its windows, embraced in thick, dark wood, looked filthier than ever. Its roof looked like it was sagging. Around its bulk wrapped a porch that she knew would warn of rather than welcome footsteps. Its front door, which Seth and Marsha had never used, loomed like a mouth.

She stepped out of the car, hoping the threat of tears would disappear as she started moving. She opened the car's back door, leaning over to pick up the pack of beers she'd bought on the way. Instinct had told her flowers, but she knew how insensitive that would have been.

She shut the door loud enough for Seth to hear, making her way toward the back of Flood House. Tire tracks marred the dry dirt. On the ground, the bright orange of the wrapper of her sister's favorite chocolate caught the sun.

"Oh, Gina," she said, shaking her head.

As the back porch greeted her, she glanced behind her at a forest that looked like it had just swallowed something. The wildness of the yard's grass matched the house, and she saw, for the first time, the edge of an old tire peeking out of its growth.

Before the guilt turned to fear, she tried the door. It opened, and she was met with stale air punctuated by forgotten food, unwashed clothes, and rooms that smelled too lived-in.

"Seth!" The house ate his name but gave nothing back.

Envelopes addressed to Marsha sat on the kitchen table. Coffee-stained cups were gathered around the sink. In the corner, a mop so dried out its head looked uncomfortably brittle stood next to a broom with a split handle.

It wasn't how Yanna would have lived but, for them, it was home. Comfort. Safety. Yanna put the beers on the table and continued into the house. The hallway stretched to the living room, bathroom, and dining room, which had been turned into a bedroom when Marsha had lost the ability to haul herself up the stairs. The door to the basement was closed.

Figuring Seth could be sleeping, she headed upstairs toward his room.

"Seth," she said, knocking lightly. "It's Yanna."

Wood swung on loud hinges. His room smelled like the kitchen but without the food. Stale. Of unwashed bedsheets, flesh, and windows that ached to be opened. Clothes were piled in corners. An open box of shotgun cartridges sat on top of a dresser, next to a photograph of him and his mother. Beside his bed: pots of painkillers and cups filled with water.

The room was his, but it was empty.

She was about to leave when something caught her eye, slipped between two cups. It was a sheet of paper, lined, and the closer she moved toward it, the more the scratches of Seth's writing became legible. She lifted it out of its makeshift filing cabinet. Unfolded it to read.

July 3: Noises in the basement. An animal? Something moving.

July 8: Table changed in the living room. Looked new.

July 15: Porch repaired. Looked new.

July 17: Dead flowers in the downstairs hallway. Mom shouting.

As she continued reading, the guilt returned, festering its way into her with barbed teeth. Yanna had noticed a change in Seth. An irritability that something was shifting, out of his control. The more she thought about it, the more it aligned with what she was reading. She had no idea it was happening so often. She had no idea it had amounted to this.

It brought her back to the first time he'd taken her up on the offer of help. Her phone had started bleating. The house had been dark, her head humming after too many drinks. Normally, she'd leave it. Put it down to a wrong number or something that could wait until morning. But something told her it would be Seth. Something told her she should go into the other room and pick it up.

"Yanna? It's Seth."

"Seth? It's like...two a.m." Her head hummed with the beers she'd finished a couple of hours ago. She sat up, enjoying the satisfaction as she rubbed her eyes.

"I know, I know. Do you think you could come over?"

"To the house?"

"Yeah, it's just...I think there's someone here."

"What? Seth, what are you doing on the phone with me? Dial 911. I'll call Gina."

"No, no, no," he said. She heard panic in his voice. "Just you."

"What?"

"Just you. No cops. Don't tell Gina. Please."

No one pulled Yanna over that night. As the streetlights swept their reflections across the top of her car, she didn't encounter a single soul. When she reached the tunnel of twisted growth that led to Flood House, the car's headlights highlighting the sharp leaves and untamed wood, she was anxious, unsettled, praying she wouldn't have to use the pistol on the passenger seat.

When she saw the kitchen light on, Seth's wide figure illuminated in its window, she breathed a sigh of relief. As she stepped onto the back porch, weapon gripped between clammy hands, he opened the door to meet her.

"You brought a gun?"

"Yes, I brought a fucking gun," Yanna snapped. She looked around, searching for a sign that someone had been here, but was only met with two worried faces and the smell of something sweet.

Marsha sat at the table, moving finger over finger. Her hair looked like a thin, wired bird's nest and worry had puffed the bags under her eyes. The T-shirt she was wearing, so big it almost draped to the floor, had a faded print of a chili pepper contest on the front.

"And why wouldn't I? You said someone was in the house."

"I shouldn't have asked you here," Seth said, releasing a labored heave. He pulled out a chair. Sat next to his mother. "I shouldn't have asked you to come."

"What? Seth, is there someone in the house or not?"

"I don't know."

"I don't understand?"

When Seth replied with silence, irritation oozed. Yanna was tired, only a handful of hours from a headache and the start of her shift at Ed's. At this point, she almost hoped there'd be something to shoot at. Sliding the safety off the gun, she left the kitchen. When Seth called out to stop her, she ignored him, pressing into the hallway.

The house was dim but she pushed on, barrel raised in front of her, heart beating so hard it hurt her chest.

She swept into every room of Flood House, turning into each like she'd seen in the movies. Upstairs was empty. The basement was empty. Every room of the house sat undisturbed and unoccupied, so when she reentered the kitchen she felt tension pressing the sides of her temples and harsh words itching to escape her teeth.

"Seth, what the hell is going on? There's no one here. Doesn't even look like there's been a break-in."

"I'm sorry," Seth muttered.

"You can be as sorry as you want, but it's not going to change the fact I hauled my ass over here for nothing."

"I said I'm sorry!" The volume caught Yanna off guard, but it was the pain that made her stop. She saw he was struggling. Really struggling. Something had him gripped, and she didn't have a chance to ask what it was before he started sobbing.

"Oh, Seth," Marsha whispered, placing a wrinkled hand on his arm. "Don't cry, honey. It's ok."

"Seth," Yanna breathed, kneeling to meet him. She wanted to ask what was wrong. Wanted him to pour it all over the table. But she waited, because she was still getting to know that Seth wasn't someone who took well to being pressed. When he was ready, he would speak.

"I..." he began, shaking his head. "It doesn't matter."

"Yes, it does. It matters."

She watched him breathe. Watched him focus on every inhale and exhale.

"You know Mom is...She's been seeing things. Hearing things."

"I do."

"That's why we moved here. Why we moved somewhere quiet."

"Oh, yes," Marsha said, her face breaking into a wide smile. "It's been a good holiday. A nice break."

Yanna returned a loving smile, squeezing Seth's shoulder to let him know she understood.

"Most nights she'll wake me up," he continued. "Get herself ready. Shout up to my room. Tell me about what she saw. Only tonight, she wasn't lying. I saw what she'd seen."

Yanna's eyebrows knitted with confusion. "What did you see?"

"A man. Outside."

"It was Joseph," Marsha interrupted, angry he'd forgotten. "The man who used to live here. The one with the flowers. I told you that."

"Alright, Mom," Seth said. "Just let me finish telling Yanna."

"Go on," Yanna urged.

"I watched him from my bedroom window. Watched him walk out from the trees right up to the house. He let himself in. Walked inside. I heard the door open, Yanna. Heard it close and heard him lock it. Someone was moving around downstairs."

"And then?"

"I went down to confront him but he was gone. I was scared. Unsettled. Didn't know what to do. Who to talk to. So, I called you."

"And I'm glad you did," Yanna said. While she tried to stay calm, a concern had started gnawing at her. She hadn't been there when Marsha had tried to pry the eyes from Kathy Waite's skull, and she hadn't been there when her sister had found her naked on Salem Road, but she'd heard what had happened.

Stillwater had had something to say about both those events, and she'd listened. Listened and chosen to act with kindness. Now, as she looked at Marsha, she tried to imagine how an old woman so sweet could attempt something so barbaric.

Did Seth have that same violence in him? Would he do something to hurt her?

"I can't tell you what you saw, but I've checked every room," Yanna said, finally. "There's no one else in this house."

"Do you believe me?" Seth asked. "Do you believe us?"

"I do," Yanna said.

"Really?"

"Really."

She rubbed a thumb across his skin. Looked away. Hoped her smile was warm enough to hide the fact she was lying.

YANNA SLID the paper back between the pill bottles. She closed her eyes, trying to exorcise all the feelings running through her head. She moved toward the window, wondering what it would be like seeing a man emerge from the forest's shadows. She wondered if Seth had mistaken the tree's trunks as limbs, or the leaves as hair.

Yanna almost wished someone would emerge. At least then there'd be some substance in all this.

When Yanna left the bedroom, she went to close the door, but something felt different. Something *looked* different.

She swore the hallway floor had been empty but now, a long, dark rug ran its length.

"What the fuck?"

She lifted her foot, staring at her shoe as though its sole would be burned. She thought back to the list of changes Seth had noted, interrogating her memories for how the hallway had looked before.

She swallowed hard, hurrying down its length as a chill rode itself through her body. A framed photograph of Seth, Marsha, and Seth's father, Sully, hit the wall as she moved past it. She screamed, and questions raced through her mind. Was that picture always hanging there? Should stairs feel this steep? Hadn't the basement door been closed?

As she pushed for the exit, questions continued like sharp incisions, stabbing until she saw something on the kitchen table that filled her with horror.

It was a bunch of flowers. Alive, not dried, stems roughly tied together with string. Around it, a couple of petals had broken off, their colors making the table's surface look dirty.

Yanna pressed her hand to her mouth. Tried to suppress the scream.

No one else had stirred in the house. No noise had made its way from downstairs. Those flowers weren't there before.

She pushed past the kitchen, drawing her limbs close in case the petals would reach out and touch her. As she did, she heard a sound behind her. A low cry, unfurling from the basement.

She looked toward it. Held her breath as the sound morphed into the heave of something shifting.

She pursued the idea of getting out. Seth didn't matter. Marsha's memory didn't matter. Flood House didn't matter. All that fueled her was the thought of getting in the car, reversing away from the place so fast her tires took a moment to catch up, and following the green tunnel until she reached air that tasted kinder, cleaner, and allowed her a moment to breathe.

"Shit," Yanna groaned, leaning over to pick up the phone, alive with a photograph of her sister with a hot dog hanging out of her mouth. She answered, the edges of a dream wearing away against the morning sun. "Hello?"

"Yan, where are you?"

"In bed. Why?"

"I'm outside."

Yanna moaned, rolling onto her back. "What time is it?"

She heard Gina's voice retreat as she pulled the phone away to answer the question. Irritated, Yanna hung up, dragging her feet to the silhouette that matched her sister's on the other side of the door.

"It stinks in here," Gina said, pushing past Yanna. Her hands rested on her gun belt, her short blond hair and sunglasses particularly reflective in the morning sun.

"I haven't had a chance to wash up."

"Been at the Kennedys' all morning trying to get a cat off their roof."

"Real police work."

"Right? God knows how it got up there or how we managed to get it down, but we did. I was in the area. Thought I'd stop by."

Yanna shared a smile, hands wrapped around her body. "Do you want coffee?"

"No, no. Can't stay long. We've got a few things to wrap up with Seth."

"You seen him today?"

"Seth? No. Why?"

Visions of last night flooded back to Yanna. Stranded flowers. Lone petals. A strange noise unfurling from the basement. She felt sick at the thought of it. Wondered if she'd ever be able to go back.

For a moment, she thought about telling her sister. Contemplated whether it would make her feel better or worse. It didn't take long for the threat of judgement to push the words back down her throat.

"I popped in to see how he was doing yesterday but he wasn't there," Yanna said. "I haven't seen him since it happened."

"Was his truck there?"

"Yeah," Yanna replied. "Alongside the trash you left all over the place."

"Excuse me?"

Yanna turned away, surprised at how easily she'd let the comment slip.

"Nothing. Forget it."

"Yanna, what's the matter with you?"

"I'm fine."

"No, you're not."

"How would you know?"

"Because I'm your sister," Gina said, defensiveness sharpening her tone. "And because it's my job to know when someone's lying to me. I know the last few days have been tough. This is a hard time for you. But don't take it out on me."

"What's your problem with him?" An unexpected frenzy was working its way through Yanna. She didn't know where it had come from, or what had triggered it, but something about it felt good.

"With who?"

"With Seth."

"I haven't got a problem with Seth," Gina said, arms crossed.

"Yes, you do. From the moment you found Marsha out on Salem Road, you've had a problem with him. When she attacked Kathy, all you did was pass judgement. Anytime I've so much as talked about him, you find a way to put him down. The whole reason I started going over there—started offering some kindness—was because no one else would."

"Oh, you're such a hero," Gina said, waving her away.

"It's not about being a hero. It's about being there when someone's hurting. When someone's alone. I thought police officers were meant to have compassion."

"Yanna, where the fuck has this come from?"

"Tell me. What is your problem with him?"

"I don't have a problem with him!"

"Gina, tell me."

"He's just weird, ok? Different. Rude. I don't know."

"What's wrong with being different?"

"Nothing's wrong with being different."

"Clearly there is."

"Yanna, stop. We're just going to have to agree to disagree. I didn't like how he handled what happened with his mother. No one did. He did nothing to look after her properly. Didn't apologize to Kathy. Didn't say anything to

Ed when it happened in *his* store. Marsha belonged in a place with proper care. A home where someone could do a real job of looking after her. Not in that old house with someone like Seth. But like I said," Gina persisted, raising her voice when Yanna tried to protest, "that's not getting in the way of my job or my judgement."

"You're pathetic," Yanna said, shaking her head.

"I'm pathetic?" Yanna could hear that she'd worked her way under Gina's skin. Finally, she'd gotten the rise she was looking for. "That's rich coming from you. The man's besotted with you. Enamored. The whole time he's been here, you've had him wrapped around your finger like some sick puppy."

"Oh, fuck you."

"I'm serious!"

"Now it makes sense," Yanna said, shaking her head. "I should have known. You're jealous you're not in the spot-light. Finally, you've found someone not paying enough attention to you."

"Jealous? Why would I be jealous? I'm just struggling to see why, if you care about him so much, you don't do some-thing about it. Why don't you stop teasing the poor guy and just fuck him?"

Yanna's mouth fell open. She managed to hold on to the words she wanted to say, able only to force the words "get out" from her throat. She pointed behind Gina at the door, tears pressing at her eyes.

"Yanna, I didn't mean—"

"I said get out!"

Gina said nothing, gritting her teeth before turning and leaving, slamming the door so hard Yanna felt the room rattle. The house settled. The silence hurt. Walls felt stained by the words they'd slung at each other.

Yanna didn't know where that had come from or how it had escalated so quickly. Didn't know if it was the stress of Marsha dying, what she'd seen last night, or knowing she still had to face Seth that had sparked those emotions, but emotions had been there, and they'd been real.

8

As Yanna yelled Seth's name through the door's gap, all she could think about was never entering Flood House again. Not after what she'd seen in there. What she'd heard in its belly. "It's Yanna!"

"Yanna?"

She breathed at the sound of his voice. Exhaled at the idea that he wasn't just alive, but that she wouldn't have to spend a minute there alone.

As he rounded the corner and stood in the room's entrance, she saw a man who was broken. A man trapped in the poisonous claws of grief.

His name escaped her lips again, so quick she failed to catch it. He ambled toward her, bare feet scratching the floorboards' dirty surfaces. When he collapsed, she tried to hold his weight up, struggling to keep him from hitting the ground until she couldn't hold him anymore and joined him on his knees.

They stayed like that a while. He sobbed and she rubbed his back and the world continued turning. His cries were loud and messy and hers brought on tears that stained his shirt.

Eventually, the shudders quieted, the sobs softened, and Seth pulled away from her embrace. He rubbed at his face, wiping the wetness from his eyes.

"Christ," he breathed. "I needed that."

"There isn't much on this earth as healthy as a good cry," Yanna replied. "Trust me, I know. Come on. Stand up. I'll make us tea."

With the help of the table and her arm, he did, and she had to hold her breath against the smell emanating from his armpits. When he found his balance, he fell back into the chair, exhausted.

"Where were you yesterday?" Yanna asked. "I came by to see how you were doing."

"I took a walk," Seth said. "Through the forest. I was gone a while."

"Right," Yanna said, concern in her voice. She moved dirty dishes into the sink, clearing rotting food into an old yogurt container, trying to find a clear space on the counter.

"Gina told me," Yanna continued, turning on the hot faucet. She let the water wash whatever sludge had started to build around the sink's edge before she filled it up, grateful for the distraction. She didn't want to think about where she was standing. What she'd seen here only hours ago. Thoughts of aged flowers bloomed in the shadows of her mind. The curve of drying petals. The ends of stalks that looked like insect legs. The more she thought about them, the more it made her feel sick.

"Yeah?"

"How were they with you?"

"I think they were ok. Honestly, it's a blur."

"And Gina?"

"Gina was fine."

"Seth," Yanna said, pausing to turn and look at him. "I know she's my sister, but that means I know how difficult she can be. How was she?"

"She can't stand me," Seth said. "None of them can."

Yanna shook her head. "Well, I can."

"And that other guy she works with. What's his name?"

"Trey."

"Yeah. *Trey.*" She heard the resentment in his voice. "What a fucking ass."

"Last I heard, they were...you know."

"Isn't he married?"

Yanna looked over her shoulder with pursed lips, moving wet fingers across them as if to zip them shut. "Look at us," she said, returning to the sink. "Gossiping. Stillwater should love us."

That brought a chuckle out of Seth, and Yanna was pleased to hear it. All the pain, uncertainty, and aching in her gut vanished, for just a second. She put her hands back in the water's warmth, transferring more dishes to its depth.

A loud thump hit the ceiling above them, disturbing dust on a light fixture that shivered. Yanna's heart leapt. Goose bumps ignited along her back. She held her breath, the cup in her hand dripping a glob of bubbles.

"Do we have company?" Yanna whispered.

"Not that I know of," Seth replied.

Yanna lowered the cup in the water. Turned to move. Was about to call out on the back of the adrenaline breaking a sweat across her shoulders when she felt Seth's hand on her elbow. She looked down at him and saw a finger held to his lips. A slight shake of his head.

"Don't," he whispered. "Give it a moment. It'll pass."

Yanna must have replied with a look of confusion because all he did was nod again, and wrap his hand around hers. It was soft and warm. An odd comfort as her wet and soapy palm grew clammy against his. They stayed in the kitchen like statues, listening with alert ears as something unwelcome moved in the room above them.

Yanna wondered if it was an animal. A stray rat that had made its way through a hole in the house. But she knew better. This was a house where doors closed and phantom flowers appeared out of nowhere.

That was when the voice started. A sound so low and muffled Yanna couldn't make out any words. That, paired with the pressure of purposeful steps, moving from one room to another, was all Yanna needed to know it wasn't an animal up there. It was human.

Suddenly, the movement stopped. Yanna waited. Seth inhaled. When a door slammed somewhere in the hallway, sending more dust into the air, Yanna released the scream that had been trapped in her lungs.

She let go of Seth's hand, running to shut the kitchen door. She pushed her back against it, fumbling her phone out of her pocket.

"Yanna, what are you doing?" Seth said, standing.

"Calling Gina."

"No, no, no. Stop!"

"Why? Seth, there's someone upstairs! She could be here in a few minutes."

"There's no one up there."

"What are you talking about?"

"Sit down," Seth said, dropping back into his seat. "Please, Yanna."

Swallowing saliva that tasted bitter, she peeled herself from the door, allowing Seth to grab her hand and guide her to the other chair.

"Ok," she breathed, wiping wet hands on her jeans.

"But you tell me what the fuck is going on or I'm out of here, and I won't be coming back."

"Honestly? I've got no idea. But that," he said, pointing a finger above him, "is not the first time that's happened. It's not the second, either."

"What was it? *Who* was it?"

"I don't know."

"You don't know?"

"No." Seth said it so firmly, with so much conviction in his eyes, that she couldn't decide whether the panic coursing through her veins was starting to settle or not.

While Seth had been talking, she'd managed to free a cigarette and lighter from her top pocket. "You mind?"

"No." Seth waved at her. "You got another?" Yanna lit the cigarette she was holding before passing it to him. She removed another, lighting it in cupped hands. "I quit when I moved here with Mom," Seth said. "But after the last few days, hell knows I need one."

"So if you don't know who it is," Yanna pushed, leaning over the table, "how did you know to leave it?"

"Because if you do, it'll go away. It'll stop and you can carry on as normal."

"Jesus, Seth. There's nothing *normal* about it."

"I know."

"How long has this been happening?"

"Since we moved in. Mom noticed it first. She saw the changes. Told me things, but, naturally, I thought she was making it up. She was sick, and I didn't have any reason to start separating her fact from fiction. But then *I* started noticing things. A change of paint color. A different chair in the living room. They were small and infrequent—flashes— but they were there."

"That wasn't a flash, Seth. That was something walking around up there."

"That doesn't happen often—not like that. But, granted, it's more than a flash."

"That time I came over. When you saw someone walk into the house."

"Yup," Seth said, releasing a mouthful of smoke. "That was the first. I know you thought I was going crazy."

"Seth, I—"

"It's alright," he said, holding a hand up. "That night, I thought I was going crazy. I guess I needed someone to verify it. Help me figure out what was and wasn't true."

"That's why you called me about the flowers as well?"

"The flowers," Seth repeated, laughing. "Now, *that*—I'd never seen anything like it. Mom had talked about them. She kept saying she'd seen those damn things around the house. You know that's what she was shouting about when your sister picked her up out on Salem Road, right? A strange man and those fucking flowers."

Yanna looked away. She stubbed out her cigarette on a dirty plate and rubbed her temples, suddenly disgusted with the taste. She thought about telling him that she'd read the list by his bed—seen her own flowers—but didn't want him to feel she'd overstepped a line. This wasn't the time to announce she'd been looking through his bedroom.

"It's not just in the house, either," Seth continued.

"What do you mean?'

"Shit happens outside too. You remember when you came over that night, we told you about a man walking from that forest," he said, pointing behind Yanna. "I saw him yesterday. That's why I was in there. I was looking for him."

"And?"

"Nothing."

"What do you think it is? I mean, do you think it's...a ghost?"

"Last I checked, I don't believe in ghosts."

"But what if it is? What if the place is haunted? You should stay somewhere else. You can spend a few nights at mine."

"Stop," Seth said, scrunching his face, waving his hands at her. "I'm not leaving on account of some spirit."

"Why?"

"Because I'm not."

"What if it hurts you?"

"It won't hurt me."

"But—"

"Yanna, I'm not leaving," Seth snapped.

"Why?"

"Because there's a good chance it had something to do with Mom dying." As he said it, a sob caught in his throat. She saw his eyes fill with tears. Noticed his cheeks flush red.

"Seth..."

"And your sister—the police—they can say it's a heart attack until they're blue in the face, but I don't believe it. I think she saw it. I think whatever haunts this place showed itself and whatever she saw killed her. I'm not leaving until I find it, Yanna. I'm not leaving until I see it myself."

9

Over the last week, she had gotten used to Seth's expressions. The way his cheeks drooped when he was listening. The way his eyebrow creased when he didn't like something. That's what she was looking at now. A drooped cheek. A creased eyebrow.

"So, we've tried talking to it," he said. "We've tried recording it. Now, you're saying we should try summoning it."

"Summoning's a strong word," Yanna said. "I'm filing this under the talking category."

"Whatever you say."

"So, are we doing this or what?" Her knees hurt against the hardness of the basement's floor. She watched Seth grumble something under his breath, grimacing as he buckled his knees to get down with her.

"Why do we have to do it down here anyway? If the place is haunted, it doesn't matter if we do it here or upstairs. A ghost's a ghost."

"Because this is where you saw the flowers, which is the most compelling of everything you said you've seen," Yanna said. She moved the Ouija board so it was in the middle of them. Placed the wooden planchette in its center. "And—" She caught the next phrase before she said it. They both knew the next words on her lips were about Marsha's dying down here.

"She would have hated this," Seth said, shaking his head. "I remember when I was a kid. My friend Dean had one of these. Found it at the back of some shed he'd broken into. When I mentioned it to her, you would have thought I'd killed someone. She did not like the idea of me messing with this stuff."

Yanna looked away, a pang of guilt tightening her chest. "Maybe we shouldn't be doing this."

"No," Seth said. "We should. We've tried everything else. Got nothing to lose by trying something different."

"You're sure?"

"I'm sure."

"Alright," Yanna said. As she readied herself, she thought about the last seven days she'd spent in Flood House, navigating its rooms, staring out its windows, walking around its interior and the surrounding forest with so much attention to the way it existed, the house could have been alive.

In a way, she believed it was. Every pipe felt like a vein. Every window an eye. Each minute in its arms felt worth exploring. Every color, grain of wood, and movement of dust was a question. A dare. A trigger that could ignite the answers she and Seth were looking for.

She'd wake up and think about it. Get in the car and drive to it. Spend the day in its embrace before heading home, getting into bed, and dreaming about it.

Flood House had, for all its tiredness, become her routine. It had eaten her everything. Consumed her soul.

She'd promised she would help Seth find out what killed his mother, and for seven days she'd kept her word.

She'd noticed a change in Seth too. In that week, Flood House had become more than a house. The more he'd grown into the idea that it had taken away his mother, the more he owned it. He vocalized it. Wore it like a well-fitting suit. To him, Flood House was a murderer. A killer wrapped in nails, baseboards, and electrical wires. He wanted to solve it. Wanted to crack it. Wanted to bring the killer down.

"So, how does this thing work? Should we light some candles or something?"

"I'm one step ahead of you," Yanna said, rooting around in the bag she'd brought with her. She removed the candles, stripping some of the wax with her fingernails so they'd fit into the stands she'd picked up at the dollar store. She shook the box of matches at Seth, striking a couple until the candles were lit. They didn't add much to the exposed bulb that already hung from the ceiling but contributed to the atmosphere.

"Alright. Now what?"

"We put our fingers on this," Yanna said. "Come on, you too. Seth? What's up?"

His face had lost some of his color. As he sat there, she wondered if he'd already seen something. Heard something she'd missed.

"What if we make contact with her?"

Yanna stopped, and all she could think about was her own mom. There had been times through her grief that she'd thought about dialing the dead, but had, for one reason or another, always talked herself out of it.

"Then we talk to her," Yanna answered. "And if we make contact with my mom, we'll talk to her too." She saw the realization enter Seth's face. The shared trauma that had just united them.

Seth nodded, placing his finger on the planchette.

"Ok." Yanna took a moment to compose herself, coughing. "My name is Yanna," she said, raising her voice. "And this is my friend, Seth. Is there anyone here with us?"

The silence was loaded. Yanna cocked her head. Seth was sitting on the floor with his eyes closed. Both listened. Both waited. Yanna felt Seth rearrange his finger on the planchette. "We've had a few things happen here that we'd like some help figuring out," Yanna continued. "Dried flowers. Noises coming from this basement." She waited again, body tense in anticipation. "And we've seen a man...Seen him walking into the forest at the back of the house. If you are that man and you can hear us, or you know who that man is, know that we only want to talk to you. We don't mean any harm."

Again, the pair waited, but all that met them was quiet. Quiet and the natural sounds of an old house moving.

"Nothing," Seth said.

"You try."

"Try what?"

"Talking."

"Why?"

"Because maybe it'll respond differently to you. You're the only one who's seen him, remember. And you saw those flowers."

"Ok...Hello. Uh, like Yanna said, we've had some weird stuff happening here. Unexplainable stuff." Yanna caught his eye and he looked away, cheeks flushing red. "If you're here, we'd really like to talk with you. Please."

Yanna checked the board. Stared at their fingers sitting

together on that tiny piece of wood. No matter how long they waited, nothing moved it. Nothing happened.

"We tried," Seth said, taking his finger back.

Yanna sighed, removing her own finger. She felt better for it, knowing now that nothing was waiting to bite it.

"Maybe there isn't anything haunting Flood House," Seth said, grabbing for support as he pushed himself to his feet. "Maybe we're all just losing our fucking minds."

SETH HAD BEEN TALKING about an apple pie his mom used to make when Yanna finally saw what was haunting Flood House standing in the yard.

She'd just told Seth she was going back to work when she'd caught movement. A different texture and color of skin against all the shivering foliage.

He didn't look like a ghost. There was no translucency of skin or aura of menace. Whoever was standing at the edge of the forest wasn't someone who looked supernatural or like it had been dragged from somewhere sinister, but she knew she was looking at the thing they'd been searching for. The presence they'd been calling on. She knew she was staring at the ghost that haunted Flood House, there when they had least expected it.

He was skinny. Yanna guessed he couldn't be older than forty. Hair hung in front of his eyes in tight, dark curls and he was wearing jeans and a white T-shirt that clung to bones defining his thin frame. She swallowed, trying hard to keep whatever sound she wanted to make in her mouth.

Of all the things she'd expected the ghost to look like. Of all the contorted faces, figures, eyes, and limbs she'd put together in her head, what confronted her was different.

This man looked normal. *Alive.* After weeks spent trying to coax him out, Yanna wanted to know what he sounded like. What he smelled like. What his pores and fingernails and eyelashes looked like up close.

The realization of it beat down on her like an endless heat. The world slowed. Seth's voice faded, replaced with a gentle hum that something was there that shouldn't be.

Then she noticed what he was holding. She saw the freshly pulled flowers in one hand, and the gun gripped in the other.

"Yanna?" Seth said. "You alright?"

All she did was nod. A slight tip of the head to the world outside.

By the time Seth noticed him, releasing a forced "fuck" from his mouth, the stranger outside had started walking, closing the distance between the edge of the forest and where they were standing.

The situation mounted, squeezing what little air she had left out of her lungs. It wasn't just her and Seth anymore. There was an anomaly here. A new presence. A new problem. She felt Seth leave the room behind her. Heard him moving across loud floorboards as she continued watching the odd man move, pistol in hand, closer to the back of Flood House.

Seth pushed past her. Shouted something Yanna didn't catch as he opened the door and stepped out onto the porch. The warm sun bounced off the side of Seth's shotgun, which he gripped tight against his body.

"Hey!" Seth yelled. "You put that gun down. Right now. You put it down or I will shoot!"

Yanna leaned against the kitchen counter. One hand gripped her own neck so hard it left red welts against her pale skin.

The strange man kept moving. Even with a shotgun pointed at him, he didn't stop. Didn't express any recognition that they were there at all. His eyes were on the house and that was where he was going. To him, Seth and Yanna were invisible. To that strange man, they didn't exist.

"This is your final warning, you son of a bitch," Seth shouted. "One more step and I blow your fucking brains out."

He took another step and Yanna winced. She saw Seth hold his breath as he pulled the trigger.

The sound of the shotgun was so loud in that tranquil space it was like it had dented the air.

Yanna expected to see blood and fragments of bone. She expected to see liquid stain the long grass, but that didn't happen. When the bullets made contact with the man's shoulder, he didn't fall forward, or backward, or limp as he should have. Instead, those bullets were transformative. As soon as they hit skin, snapping his body back with violence, flesh and bone became flowers.

The body buckled, collapsed into itself, and what lay on the ground wasn't a corpse leaking blood, but a collection of dried-out petals in dizzying colors, piled in a horrendous, pretty heap.

10

By the time Yanna reached the small town of Shiver, it had started raining. After driving under dark and oppressive clouds for close to an hour, it had been almost a relief to see her windscreen peppered with water.

As she passed the tidy garden and white picket fence, walking up a cobbled path to the red door with a bright gold knocker, she wondered if she'd gotten the right house. It had been so long since she'd been here. So many years since she'd seen her face. The last time had been at her mother's funeral, and that day had been a blur.

She knocked and waited.

Knocked again and waited some more.

When the door opened and she saw how deep the frown was burrowed into the face of the old woman in front of her, she realized why she and Gina had always called her Constantly Complaining Constance.

"Constance?"

"Who's asking?" the old woman snapped, eyebrows knitted together. Yanna tried to remember if she'd always been that tiny.

"You don't remember me," Yanna said.

"Nope."

"You knew my mother. Ida Carter."

"Ida Carter?"

She saw the name register. Saw the old woman rooting through the filing cabinets of her mind.

Those filing cabinets were why Yanna was here. Constance complained, but she listened. She'd grown up in Stillwater and, if her mother was right, there wasn't much she missed.

"Shit, how old we've grown," Constance said. "Gina." She pointed a finger at Yanna, firm look still on her face. "That's it. I remember now. Last I heard, you were training to be a cop or something. You don't look like a cop. What in all hell are you doing out here?"

"I wanted to ask you a few questions," Yanna said, deciding the wrong name and profession could work to her advantage.

"About?"

"An investigation we've got going on in Stillwater," Yanna said.

Constance scrunched her nose up at the place's name. Looked Yanna up and down.

"Alright," the old woman muttered, turning inside. "But I haven't got long. My show starts in less than an hour, and you won't be making me miss it. Linda did that last week, and I won't let it happen again. Take those shoes off when you come in too. I hate to think what you people have stepped in."

The air in Constance's house was heavy with the smell of fried onions. A cup of coffee was steaming on a table in the living room beside an overweight cat.

"I don't know how helpful I'm going to be," Constance

announced, falling into the armchair's groove. "And honestly, I don't know how helpful I *want* to be. All you lot seem to do is get it wrong. Tax money straight down the drain, if you ask me."

Yanna perched on the sofa's edge.

"Flood House," Yanna said, cutting to the chase.

Yanna noted Constance pause. Watched her relive something she hadn't considered for a long time.

"What about it?"

"We're doing some research into its history. Into who used to live there."

"Only people I ever saw living there were the Lethes," Constance replied, folding thin arms across her skinny body. "Most recently, Joseph Lethe. Raised by his grandmother. Stayed there after she died. He was quiet. Weird."

"Weird, how?"

"Oh, I don't know. Just something off about him. People thought he had something to do with that young girl who disappeared, but I don't know if I believe that."

"Which girl?"

"You know the one," Constance said, rotating her wrist in the hopes it would dislodge the name from wherever it had gotten stuck. "And if you don't, shame on you. It was all over the news. Had Stillwater in a chokehold. Debra Garcia. That's it. My God, that poor girl. Even saying her name gives me goose bumps. And to think they never found her. Like I said." She pointed a shaking finger at Yanna. "Tax money down the damned drain."

Something about the name felt familiar. Perhaps, in her youth, she'd heard it before. Stillwater wasn't a place where people went missing. She could imagine how much of a stir it would cause.

"And people said the person who lived there—Joseph?"

"Joseph Lethe, yes."

"They think he had something to do with it?"

"Oh, that was just gossip. Rumors. You know what people in Stillwater are like. They don't like odd, so it made sense in their heads. Personally, I think it's a bit extreme, but if you're that concerned about it, you should just ask him."

"Ask who?"

"Joseph!"

"What do you mean, ask him?"

"For a cop, you're terrible at your job."

"Tell me."

Constance sighed.

"Last I heard, he's alive," Constance continued, brushing down her beige pants. Yanna thought back to the man they'd seen at Flood House. The man who had haunted its hallways, who had walked toward them clutching a pistol before erupting into flowers. She wondered if it was the same man she was talking about. Wondered if his name was Joseph Lethe.

"Joseph Lethe is alive?"

"Yes, ma'am. Living and breathing out in that dump they call Hunt."

YANNA WAS SITTING in her living room. Jam reflected light from her laptop on bread Ed had insisted she take home. He said he was worried she wasn't eating, and he was right. She couldn't remember the last time she had eaten a home-cooked meal.

Yanna moved her fingers over the trackpad. Brought up

another archived newspaper report from 1983 as crumbs got lost between letters on her keyboard.

"Lonegrove girl still missing," she murmured to herself. "Police are continuing their search for Debra Garcia, the nineteen-year-old girl from Lonegrove pronounced missing last Thursday. Debra, lovingly dubbed 'Popcorn' by her friends, attended a party in the Stillwater area but didn't return home. Police are asking anyone with information to come forward."

The surface of the trackpad whispered as she separated her fingers, zooming into the photograph of Debra's face. She was young. Smiling. Her face filled with the possibility of future.

She opened another tab, typing Debra Garcia's name and Stillwater for what felt like the hundredth time that night. Yanna had been sitting like that for hours. Clicking. Zooming. Reading. Trying to piece together the parts of a time that had, as Constance promised, ensnared Stillwater in a chokehold.

After reading another article that featured an interview with Debra's mother, she opened another tab. Typed another name.

Joseph Lethe.

It was a unique name, but even that didn't reveal any clues. The more pages she clicked through, the more obituaries she uncovered, and the less she was filled with hope.

She tried again, adding Hunt to the search.

It was on the second page that she found a website for a place in the small town. A bingo hall that, judging from the reviews and photographs, looked like it needed a fresh lick of paint. It led her to a collection of winners, where those lucky enough to have their numbers come up posed with a smile, piece of paper and winning bingo pen in hand.

She brought up the search shortcut. Typed Joseph's name into the little box.

"Oh my God," Yanna breathed. She felt the color drain from her face. Felt a damp cold flush her system. Yanna tried to process what she was looking at. She released her fingers on the trackpad, zooming into the image the search had jumped to.

In the photograph, he was older, wearing a bomber jacket so faded he must have owned it for years. He was smiling, sitting at a table, one hand gripping a bingo dauber, the other on top of a grid of numbers stained with dark, ominous ink.

His dark hair had grown gray and thin, swept to the back of his head, and he sported a beard that was broken and unruly around the bottom of his long face. The person in the photo was aged—an old man—but there was no doubt who she was looking at.

This was the man in the yard.

The man she'd seen at Flood House.

Joseph Lethe. The man Seth had shot and turned into flowers.

11

Yanna told Seth everything.

She shared what she had heard at Constance's. She shared everything she'd found about Debra Garcia. She talked about the newspaper clippings, appeals for information, and the fact her friends called her Popcorn while he stood listening, surrounded by piles of his mother's clothes at the top of Flood House, absorbing every word like a sponge.

Then she'd told him about the photograph of Joseph Lethe.

"Joseph Lethe," Seth had repeated. It was like he was tasting it—savoring the name on his tongue—but as soon as the "Lethe" left his mouth, a muffled sound reached them from somewhere in the bowels of Flood House.

"Did you hear that?" Yanna whispered.

Seth nodded, putting a finger to his lips.

Yanna tried to latch on to it. There was something human about it. Something sad. The more she listened, the more she understood she was hearing faint and muffled sobs.

Seth left the bedroom on slow feet. He leaned over the banister as Yanna tried to mold the shape of the sounds into syllables or words. He looked over his shoulder. Shook his head to announce the coast was clear before beckoning Yanna to follow.

They moved meticulously, managing their weight down to the ground floor. As they reached it, the voices stopped. Yanna and Seth stood still, nerves suspended in an atmosphere that felt oppressive and heavy.

"That door was closed when I got here," Yanna whispered, pointing to the basement's entrance, voice as quiet as she could make it.

"You're sure?"

Yanna nodded and Seth moved toward it, treading on careful feet until he stood next to the door's frame. As he peered inside, sound swelled out on the back of a smell that was dark and damp.

"You gotta eat," the first voice said. It sounded tired. Yanna could tell it belonged to a man.

As another voice emerged from that basement, Yanna's heart started thumping so hard she wondered whether whoever was down there would hear it.

It was a woman's. Young. Scared. Asking whether she could go home.

⸺

DEBRA GARCIA WATCHED the question settle. Watched the damp air eat it up. In front of her sat a bowl of popcorn she knew she wasn't going to eat, no matter how good it smelled. Above her, countless bunches of dried flowers hung like corpses, thin limbs tied together with string.

The man who'd brought her here stared in disappointment, dark hair a shocking contrast to his white T-shirt.

"No. You cannot go home," he muttered. She noted a sadness on his face and almost felt something for him—sorry that she'd just let him down. "But try and eat," he continued. "I read in the paper they call you Popcorn, so I know you like it."

She lifted her head at what she'd just heard. If she was in the paper, they knew she was missing. If he knew about the popcorn, someone had spoken to her friends. To her family. Her heart reached out to the hope. Her whole body ached with it.

All she had to do was wait. Just stay alive a little longer.

She thought back to the moments that had led her here.

The sounds of the party had been ringing in her ears, its smell lingering on her clothes. Her skin had been warm with the same alcohol that made her mouth taste like metal. The night had been sticky. She'd had the vehicle's window down. If she wasn't dealing with the sickness of falling in love, she might have enjoyed the cool breeze against her face.

"It's Melody, isn't it?" Bradley had asked, taking his eyes off the road to look at her. "It's because she was there."

"I dunno," Debra had said.

"Is it? Deb, tell me."

"Do you still like her?"

She remembered Bradley releasing a noise between laughter and spitting before wiping the spray from his mouth in embarrassment. "No."

"Why are you lying?"

"I'm not lying!"

"Brad, I see the way you look at her. The way you stand

when you're talking with her. Everyone sees it. Even Hayley said something."

When he'd denied it again she'd asked him to stop the car. She hadn't just asked. She'd shouted it. Screamed it. *Let me out of this fucking car.*

So he did. He slammed his foot into the pedal and stopped the vehicle.

"What the fuck are you doing?"

"Walking," Debra had said, lifting herself out.

"From here to Lonegrove? You got any idea how long that'll take?"

"I don't care."

"Do you know how dark it gets out here? What if you run into someone?"

"I don't care!" Debra had shouted it, shutting the car's door with a slam. In that moment, she didn't care. Didn't care if she met someone. Didn't care if the dark drowned her. In that moment, she cared about nothing but getting away from a boyfriend who didn't show her respect.

Then the car had pulled away, the black had closed in around her, and every part of Debra wished he had stayed. She wished she hadn't said anything about Melody, and she wished Bradley had put up more of a fight. As she saw the car disappear, taking a corner in the road, she realized how right he'd been, and how dark those trees could get.

It hadn't been long before light had split around the trees, making their trunks look thick and monolithic. Debra had breathed a sigh of relief, happy that Bradley had decided to turn back.

Only, the closer the vehicle drew, the more it dawned on her that it wasn't Bradley. As the car weaved its way around the road in the direction of the party, the shadows shifted into a station wagon, older and louder than the vehicle Bradley's parents had gifted him for his eighteenth birthday. The engine and tires sounded different. The color was different. Nothing about this car was the same.

As it shone its headlights directly at her, she'd noted the moment the driver saw her, even if she couldn't see his face.

"You alright, miss?"

The voice had been clear, with enough concern in it that Debra had stopped walking. She remembered leaning over slightly to peer inside the car. She was looking at a man who was skinny, alone, with dark and messy hair. He was older than her.

"Oh, I'm fine," she'd replied, hugging herself against the loneliness and the dark. "Thanks. My boyfriend's just on the way to pick me up. He'll be here any minute."

"I see," the man had said. "That wouldn't be the same boyfriend I saw driving the other way, would it? He was going fast. Nearly ran me off the road." Debra didn't answer, but she could sense the man looking at her, waiting on an answer. "I don't know what's going on and quite frankly it's none of my business," he continued. "But it's going to take you close to an hour to get anywhere in Still-water worth getting to. In this old thing, I could get you there in five minutes." When she said nothing he leaned over the seat to get a better look at her, tilting his head. "If that *was* your boyfriend back there, it didn't look like he was coming back."

"I don't know," Debra said. She shuffled on her feet, aware of the road's hard texture and a throbbing blister on her foot. Her parents had told her not to get into cars with strangers, but this was a small town. Hayley said Stillwater was boring. Nothing like that happened here. What could go wrong in five minutes?

"I'm pretty sure where I need to go is the other way," she said, buying time.

"Don't worry about that. It's a few minutes out of my night to make sure a young lady is safe. If it was my little sister out here, I'd want someone to do the same with her."

"You've got a sister?"

"Sure do. Nancy, her name is. Don't get to see her as much as I'd like. Moved on out of here to somewhere colder with her boyfriend. He's nice, though. I reckon she'll be married in the next few years."

That's what did it. Somehow, knowing that this stranger had a sister made it safer. Made getting into a stranger's car more plausible.

Within seconds of getting in, she knew she'd made a mistake. She'd sensed it as soon as they started driving. She'd thought about opening the door and rolling out, but a gun had appeared in the man's hand and all she could do was listen. Wait as she was taken to a house with a porch that wrapped its body like a cocoon and forced to enter a damp and lonely basement, where her hands were tied behind her back to a cold metal pipe that wouldn't shift no matter how hard she shook it.

"Please," she whispered, pushing the memory away.

The tears she thought had run out started moving again. She sobbed against the anxiety stepping on her chest. "I won't tell anyone," she pleaded. "I won't tell a soul. If you let me go, I won't tell anybody about anything. *Please.*"

The man let out a sigh. Shook his head.

"I can't do that."

"Hey!" Debra shouted as the man turned to leave. "Listen to me!"

"Shhh," the man said, easing her down with his hands. "Stop your shouting. My head is pounding."

"Stop my shouting?" Debra felt the desperation harden to anger. She felt the helplessness rework itself into action. She kept shouting, using it to funnel the venom that had been festering in her soul. "You've got me down here, tied to a fucking metal pipe with all these disgusting, dead flowers hanging from the ceiling. And you expect me to stop shouting? You expect me to stop *fucking* shouting?"

The strange man stared at her. She didn't know if she expected him to get physical, violent, take that gun out from wherever it was hiding, or just shout back. When he did none of those things, only brushed dirt off his jeans and crouched in front of her, she realized death may have been better. As she looked into the eyes of the man who'd abducted her, she wondered whether ending her life would have been a sweet release.

"I told you once, and I'll tell you again. No, you cannot go home."

Debra yelped, lowering her head.

"What are you going to do to me?"

As she sobbed, she felt a finger under her chin. The man lifted it, and she met eyes that were cold and calculated.

"I'm going to put you with those flowers," he said. "You're going to look so good together."

* * *

JOSEPH LETHE, Debra Garcia, and all the suffering packed into that small space disappeared. Yanna's chest tightened. Seth's face had grown an odd shade of pale.

The room that was once full stood empty.

"Where did they go?" Yanna whispered.

"I don't know," Seth said, voice shaking. "What the fuck was that?"

Yanna had been about to declare that she didn't know, instinct ready to give the easiest and most plausible answer, but something in her gut told her she did know.

What they'd just witnessed was painful and uncomfortable, but it had unlocked something in Yanna. It was the final piece of the puzzle and all the conversations, waiting, and instances that had happened before slotted together in a bizarre, brilliant, and beautifully haunting answer.

"I think I know what's happening here," Yanna breathed, pushing the sweaty palms of her hands together. She caught Seth's eye. Saw so much hope and hurt in them she thought she might cry. She dug her nail into her finger to the point of pain, just so she could feel something. "I think I know what's going on."

"What is it?" Seth said. "What's happening?"

"I..."

"Tell me."

"I don't think Flood House is haunted by a ghost. I think it's haunted by its past."

"What do you mean?"

"Think about everything we've seen. The flowers. The man in the yard. Whatever that was. When they happen, we can see them. But they can't see us. They're completely unaware we're here."

"Right," Seth said.

"I don't think they're ghosts. I think they're memories, Seth. I think Flood House is showing us its past. Moments that have already happened. I wouldn't be surprised if Marsha saw something like what we just saw, and the sight of it scared her to death." Seth looked at her blankly, trying to process what he'd just heard.

"My God," he muttered. He put his head in his hand. Rubbed hard at his temples. "I think you might be right."

Yanna closed her eyes. Felt sadness roll a single tear down her cheek. "I think I might be too."

12

YANNA WAS familiar with the police station's noise. The talking, laughing, and clicking of computers. She still didn't know whether she liked or loathed it. It was something about the uniforms. The banter and hollow praise. The overwhelming smell of plastic.

"She in?" Yanna asked, tapping impatient fingers on the front desk.

"She is," the young man said, the mint of his chewing gum so strong it reached her. "She just got back. Should be in her office."

"Alright."

"Hey, I'm sorry about Marsha. Gina said you were close."

"Yeah, thanks," Yanna said.

She traversed the station's familiar corridors, tracing paths she'd taken before around corkboards and wastepaper baskets. She passed other rooms with blinds pulled across glass and desks littered with dirty cups, wondering again whether this was a conversation better delivered over the phone.

Those that passed her acknowledged her with a nod or a polite hello, looking at her as though she'd lost her mother again. She wondered if they knew her name, or whether she was forever branded "Gina's sister."

Finally, she arrived at Gina's office, a room that reflected her sister's personality in its orderliness, cleanliness, and dull interior. She saw surprise on her sister's face as she beckoned her in with a frantic hand.

"You bring me lunch?"

"No," Yanna said, closing the door behind her. "I was hoping we could talk."

"Alright," Gina said, hesitation in her voice. "If this is about our fight the other morning."

"It's not," Yanna said. She sat in the chair in front of Gina's desk. Gina perched on the desk's corner, hands planted on knees that stretched her pants. Yanna had forgotten what Gina looked like without her uniform. The fabric of the force—its utility belt, radio, and pistol—had become part of her skin.

"So, what's up?"

"Debra Garcia."

"What about her?"

"Do you know who she is?"

"Of course," Gina said, leaning back, crossing her arms. "Wouldn't be a good cop if I didn't."

"What about Joseph Lethe?"

"Never heard of him."

"He used to live here. In Stillwater. He lived in Flood House."

"Ok? Yanna, why are you telling me this?"

"I think he had something to do with Debra's disappearance."

"What?"

Yanna closed her eyes, steeling herself for whatever outburst Gina was hiding behind the impatient look on her face.

"I said I think Joseph Lethe had—"

"I know what you said, but I don't understand where any of this has come from."

"We found something at the house. At Flood House. We saw something."

"Who's we?"

"Me and Seth," Yanna said, watching as Gina's lip curled with disappointment.

"What did you find?"

"Nothing concrete."

"So, what then?"

"It's more...supernatural than anything else."

As Yanna began that sentence, she knew it was going to end badly. When Gina laughed, throwing her head back and releasing a cackle, Yanna knew how differently the death of their mother had impacted them. How it had shaped them. What grew between them in that laugh was an expanse of years of unsaid thoughts and feelings. A chasm in the atmosphere pulled apart by grief.

"Supernatural? Oh my God, Yanna. Someone said you'd been spending a lot of time up there, but I was *not* expecting that."

"Gina, I'm serious. We saw a vision—"

"Ok, ok, ok," Gina said, holding up both hands. "I'm going to stop you there, and I want you to listen very carefully to what I'm about to say. You have to *drop* this. I don't know what you and Seth have been doing up there, but whatever it is and whatever you think you've found, I don't want any part in it. Ok?"

"Gina, why are you like this? Why can't you listen to what I'm saying?"

"Because you're talking shit, Yanna! Visions? The supernatural? Listen to yourself."

"What about Debra Garcia?" Yanna tried one more time.

"What about her?"

"She was a real person. She's still missing. Her family is still suffering. They never found her!"

"Just what is it about him?"

"Who?"

"Seth. Only days ago his mom died and now you're here thinking you've both solved a Lonegrove disappearance. What is it about him that's got you so wrapped up in all this?"

"This has nothing to do with Seth."

"Yes, it does. All of it does. His mom hurting Kathy. Her having a heart attack. You in here, talking about ghosts. It's just...crazy, Yanna. *He* is crazy."

"Do you remember when Mom died? How everyone treated us?"

"Oh, Yanna. Stop!"

"Do you? Didn't matter if I was working the store or getting gas, people were either scared of me, or they wanted to fix me. They didn't look at me like they looked at you. They didn't treat *you* like that," Yanna shouted. She looked to see if Gina was taking it in. If she was listening. "When Seth arrived, he didn't know any of that. For the first time, I could spend time with someone who didn't make me feel like her death was part of my personality."

Gina ran her tongue along her top teeth. Nodded. Leaned in to deliver her next words as a harsh whisper. "Yanna. Do you have *evidence* that a man called Joseph

Lethe had anything to do with the disappearance of a young woman called Debra Garcia?"

"No—"

"So stop."

"Did you even hear what I just said?"

"No, Yanna. Stop! I...I just can't take this on. I have other stuff to be worrying about. Real problems in the real world."

Frustration coursed through Yanna. She should have expected it. Should have known that Gina would harden herself again and cut her off so easily. Yanna's face was hot. Her fingers fizzled with a relentless anxiety she wanted to pour out all over the table.

"I'm going to go see him."

"Who?"

"Joseph Lethe. He's alive in Hunt and I'm going to find him. I'm going to go see him and I'm going to ask him what he did to Debra Garcia," Yanna pressed, standing up.

"You can't do that."

"Why not?"

"Because I fucking said so," Gina said, shooting a glance to the glass behind her. "And because you have no idea what you're doing."

To that, Yanna scoffed. Didn't matter if they were arguing about renting an apartment in Stillwater or figuring out what haunted a house, the mantra was the same. Yanna had no idea what she was doing.

She shook her head. Left the room. Ignored the sound of her sister yelling, shouting that she didn't want any part in whatever stupid idea Yanna had planned.

13

As Yanna entered Flood House, she met a smell that was floral, but not from flowers. This was artificial. An aroma of roses, vanilla, and something edible. Something sweet.

Dirty plates and cutlery had reappeared on the counters. Unopened letters still waited on the table. Then she noticed the oven was on, its light struggling to suppress the brightness around it. She opened it, dipping her head inside to see an apple pie partway through baking.

"Wow," Yanna whispered. She was about to shout out—tell Seth how excited she was to try it—when she heard sobbing.

The cries reached her from somewhere in the house, faint and fleeting. Her mind went to Debra tied up in the basement, but the more the adrenaline subsided, and the hammering of her heart softened, the more she realized who they belonged to. These weren't the sounds of a woman. These were cries she knew.

She saw the door to the basement open. Yanna moved toward it, noting how the bulb's light met the sun on tired floorboards. It only took a few steps until the wide mass of Seth's back revealed itself.

He was on his knees. His head was in his hands and his shoulders were shaking.

"Seth," she said, moving down to meet him. "What are you doing down here?"

She rested a comforting hand on his shoulder, feeling the agitated burn of his skin.

A photograph of Marsha rested on the floor. A bottle of cheap perfume lay half empty on its side, answering whatever she could smell upstairs. Yanna didn't have to work hard to put the pieces together.

"I just wanted to see her again," he said, sitting back on his heels. "I thought if the house smelled like her—if it was reminded of her—it would show me something. If it can show us flowers and Debra and Joseph and all that horrible shit, why can't it show me Mom?"

"Come on," Yanna said, standing up. "Let's go upstairs."

"No," Seth whispered.

"Come on," Yanna persisted.

To her surprise, Seth listened, following her up to the kitchen.

Then they talked while they ate apple pie. Not about the house, Joseph Lethe, or lilies and magnolias, but about Marsha, and about Yanna's mother too. About the good times. The tough times. About all the things he missed and had loved about her.

It felt good for Yanna. For Seth. For a moment, they grieved, and Yanna could be the person she wished she'd had when her own mother was taken.

Soon, daylight died. Night took its place, and with it, conversation turned back to what it always did: Flood House.

"I'm going to find Joseph," Yanna said.

"What?"

"I'm going to find Joseph," Yanna repeated. "Gina won't help us, so I'm going to talk with him myself."

"Do you know where he lives?"

"No, but Hunt isn't huge. I'll find him."

"Let me help you."

"No," Yanna said. "You don't need to do that."

"But I want to."

"I know you do, but you shouldn't put yourself through that. Not now."

"Why not?"

"Because it's all so raw. For you, it's too emotional. Too personal."

"Damn right it's personal. This is all his fault. He didn't just kill that poor girl down there. He did something so bad the recollection of it killed Mom."

Yanna raised an "I told you so" eyebrow.

"Whatever," he grumbled, throwing a hand at her. "What would you say to him anyway? What is it you're hoping to get out of it?"

"I don't know." Yanna shrugged. "A confession. Admittance. Some sort of justice. Part of me just wants to look him in the eyes and ask why."

"That's if he even did it."

"He did do it. Of course he did. A young girl went missing and we're seeing her tied up in the basement. There's coincidence, and then there's coincidence, Seth."

Seth grunted. "But we still don't know the full story. We don't know *everything* that happened here."

It was true. Yanna didn't know everything. Didn't know why Joseph Lethe did it. How he killed her, if he did. Didn't know enough to storm into a stranger's house and start accusing him of murder. There were gaps they needed to fill. Moments that needed an answer.

But what she did know was that the answer festered in Flood House. Somewhere, within its walls, the truth nestled, waiting.

"What you were doing before I got here," Yanna began again, gently.

"What about it?" Seth looked away, embarrassment flushing his cheeks.

"It was smart. Trying to call on memories like that. I can see why you did it."

"The more I think about it, the more stupid I feel."

"Do you have any popcorn?"

"What?"

"In the house. Do you have any popcorn?"

"I don't know. Maybe? Why?"

Yanna stood, moving toward one of the cupboards next to the sink that she knew was home to chips and crackers. She opened it, moving the packets around loudly. "Would it be in here?"

"Yanna, what? No, no. If we *do* have some, it'll be in there," he said, pointing. "But I really don't know why you want that now."

Seth pushed himself to his feet, shuffling to another cupboard next to the fridge. He opened it, moving half-empty packets of rice and pasta with loud sighs. Finally, he turned with a flat bag of kernels wrapped in plastic.

Yanna took it. Tore the plastic and moved the bag to the microwave.

"Yanna, what are you doing?"

"The newspaper reports. The clippings. Debra's friends called her Popcorn."

"So?"

"And the first time we saw her in the basement she had a bowl of it in front of her. Remember?" Yanna closed the microwave's door with a slam. The numbers beeped as she pressed them.

"You're fucking crazy." Seth said, realization pouring onto his face.

Yanna pushed the START button with her thumb. The microwave whirred, loud and aggressive, spinning the flat bag until it expanded like a lung.

14

Debra's head ached. The ropes that bound her wrists had created marks so raw they throbbed every time she moved. Her throat was sore from shouting, and her mouth was so dry it had forgotten the taste of water.

Above her, flowers shivered against the impact of feet on floorboards. She traced the man's movements, eyes raised to a ceiling thick with splinters. She knew when he'd reached the top of the basement stairs. She braced herself as the sound of the door unlocking echoed down to her with short metal snaps.

She saw his shoes and then the bottom of his pants. Saw his skinny waist and the thin belt struggling to keep everything together. She smelled the bowl of popcorn before she saw it, gripped between thin fingers.

"Morning," he said, putting the bowl in front of her, next to a glass of water that had started collecting dust. Oil stained his front. Dirt clung to the tips of his shoes. After he'd set the bowl on the floor, he threw the dishcloth he'd been holding over his shoulder. "What do you say we try and eat something today? Drink something?"

Debra brought her knees under her chin. She looked to the floor, ashamed of how strongly she could smell herself.

"Alright," Joseph continued. "I'll tell you what. If I untie you for a couple minutes—give those wrists of yours a rest—you'll drink and eat something for me. How does that sound?"

The idea sounded so euphoric it awoke something in Debra, and for the first time in what felt like forever, she sensed a stirring in her gut. A stirring that said it was ok to keep going. There was an exit here.

The words caught on the dryness of her throat. She coughed. Tried again. "You'd do that?"

"I would." Joseph nodded. "But only if you promise to drink. All flowers need water."

"Ok," Debra whispered.

He reached a hand behind his back, revealing the pistol tucked in his jeans. It brought her back to the first time she'd seen a weapon. Her friend Avery had claimed that introduction, taking her into the garage to reveal the pistol her dad purchased after their house had been broken into. Avery had asked if Debra wanted to hold it. She hadn't, but said yes anyway. It took her a while to forget how heavy it was. How much empowerment she'd found in its bullets and trigger.

"I'm going to untie you," he said. "If you try anything, if you attempt to get away, I will kill you. Do you understand?"

Debra nodded. Her heart ached. As his scent filled her nostrils and relief flushed her wrists, she knew this was her opportunity. If she was ever going to get out of this hell of a house, it was now.

When she leaned back and forced her foot into his face, as hard as she'd ever forced anything in her life, she didn't expect the pistol to go off. Didn't expect the sound to fill up so much space in that room.

The darkness ignited. Her ears rang with it, and she had no idea what had happened to the bullet. She screamed, checking herself for blood, patting down her body, waiting for the adrenaline to give way to pain. Only, it never arrived. No wound revealed itself, and it turned out only one of them was bleeding.

His mouth was filled with it, blooming red against a lip she'd kicked into his bottom teeth. She scrambled, willing her arms and legs to pick up her weight and carry her across a room that felt like an ocean to the basement's stairs, where she'd fly up and out of this house, this prison, out into the world so she could scream and shout for people that loved her enough to call her Popcorn.

She lunged herself at the idea. Spent every morsel of energy left in her body on getting out. Her foot knocked over the water. It hit the first step, the second. She skipped the third to land on the fourth. The light around her shifted. The air tasted cleaner. The top of the house was in sight. She dared to look back at Joseph and saw...

***

HE WAS TOO CLOSE. It was the gun that had gone off. The shot that had filled Flood House's basement with a sound so violent it made Yanna's ears sting. Debra shouldn't have spent time patting down her body. She shouldn't have waited to see if she was bleeding.

Joseph was quick. He caught up with Debra before she'd even made it halfway up the stairs. He grabbed at her ankle, pulling her legs from under her.

Debra landed so hard on her chest that she wheezed,

crying out at fingers that failed to break her fall. Yanna put her hand to her mouth, looking over at Seth gripping his own hands in clammy nervousness.

They'd waited days for something like this, tried everything they could to coax the haunting out of wherever it was hiding. In the end, it was the smell of popcorn that did it.

This should have been a moment to celebrate, but Yanna felt dirty, like they were watching something personal, sacred, that they didn't have permission to see.

In front of them, Debra and Joseph struggled in a tangle of strained breaths and limbs. The young girl screamed, shouting for help as loudly and desperately as a hurt person could toward a door that must have looked like an oasis. Joseph pulled on her legs again, trying to unstick her fingers from where they were gripped around one of the wooden stairs. The wood cracked, the sound so loud it was like another gunshot. She saw a sliver of it gripped in Debra's hand as she rolled backward with Joseph onto the basement floor.

"Stop!" Joseph yelled. Blood flew from his lips. He aimed the pistol toward Debra, hands shaking. "You stop, or I swear to God, I will shoot you."

If Yanna didn't know it was a memory, she would have believed these were real people in front of her. She saw the blood on Joseph's lip. The dust dislodged in the air. The grain in the sliver of wood Debra was holding.

Yanna wondered if Debra would go for it again. Part of her wanted to shout at her to do it.

Run.

Escape.

Plunge that wood into his neck and get out.

But before Yanna had decided whether she was going to shout or not, the vision ended.

The blood, dust, and wood were ripped away. Debra and Joseph were gone, and she was left standing next to Seth feeling nothing but sadness in a damp and neglected basement.

15

THEY'D BEEN outside when Seth voiced the idea, looking at the dense expanse of leaves slowly swallowed by dusk.

"It's in the flowers," he'd said, taking a long sip of beer.

"What is?"

"The answer to what happened here. To why that monster did what he did. I can feel it."

"You think?"

"I know."

"What do you think we should do about it?"

"We make the house remember. We hang our own flowers. Bring them in. Dry them out. We force it back to the moment Joseph Lethe did whatever it is he did to that poor girl."

"You think that'll work?"

"What you did with the popcorn was nothing short of wild, but it got something moving. Those flowers are always there. Watching. They're an important part of what happened."

Yanna downed her own beer, thinking of them. He was

right. For all they'd seen in the last weeks at Flood House, those flowers had been a constant. They'd always been there, lurking above them like brittle eyes.

"Alright." She nodded.

"Alright," he echoed.

"I guess we should get to work."

It took four days for them to fill every surface of every room with flowers. Foxglove sat next to yarrows. Countertops were coated with trillium, and armchairs gave rest to roses. Yanna gathered what flowers she could from Ed's, securing them before they were thrown out, and Seth ventured into the forest, preferring to pull them wild.

For four days, they didn't leave Flood House without bringing beauty back into it.

When Seth returned to the house on that fourth evening clutching daisies, announcing they had enough, they started bringing them into bunches. They tied sticky stems together with string, curating petal shape and color in the hopes it would summon a man capable of kidnapping a young woman from Lonegrove.

One evening, flowers spread around her like a floral skirt, Yanna had stopped and considered the horror of what they were doing. These weren't flowers for her. They weren't for Seth or Marsha. All this was for a stranger. A monster who'd kept a young woman tied up in the basement.

More than once, she'd wondered whether she wanted any of it. Whether she should just leave the basement, the house, and Stillwater, but every time, she went back to Debra's face. The desperation in her screams and the tears on her cheeks. She imagined herself tied to the basement's pipe, raw skin burning around her wrists.

Every time doubt loomed its head, it wasn't Marsha or Seth that kept her steady. It was Debra.

When they had enough bunches, they brought them into the basement, carrying them with careful hands, arranging them in rows on the floor, ready for hanging.

"I don't know whether this is the most beautiful thing I've ever seen, or the most haunting," Yanna said, standing back from the pile with hands on hips. Seth was busy at the room's other side, attaching the first bunch of daisies and hydrangeas to the ceiling's exposed wood.

"I'm going with haunting," Seth wheezed.

"Do you still think this is going to work?"

"It better. My fingers are sticky, my back is killing me, and the smell of it all is already making me feel sick."

He put his arms down with a loud huff, taking his own step back from the flowers. They hung like drops of water, string coiling from their stems like a pig's tail.

Yanna joined him. She reached a hand up to them, brushing a finger against the lowest petals. "It's a shame," she said quietly. "How helpless they look."

She pushed the thought away. Picked up her own ball of string from the shelving unit Seth had placed it on. Gathered the scissors and a handful of nails so she could start working on the room's other side.

Then they'd started hanging them, one after the other, attaching what was once living to the same wood Joseph had dented years ago.

Throughout, Yanna expected Joseph to appear. She was prepared to turn and see him standing in the basement holding a pistol, or hear a new weight on basement stairs, but in the time it took them to smother the ceiling with blooms, they heard nothing. No one appeared in the basement. No cries or sobs marred the air. It was like Flood House was watching. Waiting for the right moment to reveal its secrets.

By the time they were done, the afternoon had turned to evening and Yanna had created something so alive, wild, and captivating, she believed she could be a god.

"I wonder how it feels," Seth said, making her mortal again.

"How what feels?"

"Flood House. Being forced to face its trauma like this."

Yanna contemplated it. Reflected on her own horrors and hauntings, trying to think of all the memories she didn't want to go back to, and how she would feel if people were forcing her to relive them.

"I guess I never thought of it like that."

"I don't know how I'd feel if someone forced me to watch Mom die again," Seth said, head down. "Someone should only ever have to go through something like that once."

"Right," Yanna whispered.

Seth sighed. She heard him swallow and wondered if he was trying to suppress stress or tears. Suddenly, the flowers felt ominous. Oppressive. What had been impressive minutes ago was now tainted and parasitic. An unnatural presence in a dark basement.

She had lost count of the number of websites she'd scrolled, reading about hanging them up and drying them out. She learned that they would look better in the dark. That they would keep their color if you kept them out of the sun. She had wanted to do the job right. Wanted to hang them well. Now, all she wanted to do was watch them burn.

"So, what do we do now?" Yanna asked.

"We wait for them to dry out."

"That could take days. Weeks."

"So we wait for weeks," Seth said.

And while they hardly talked in those weeks, and the tides of their emotions churned with anticipation, hope, and dread, wait for weeks they did.

16

For the last hour, Debra had watched him admire them, moving methodically from one bunch to the next, progressing only when he was satisfied each petal was hanging as he wanted it.

If he was in pain after their struggle, he didn't show it. If he was nervous, she didn't know. Her chest ached from where she'd fallen, and she was positive two of her fingers were broken. She didn't have to watch him to know she'd come out worse than he had.

After she'd kicked him in the face and found herself looking down the dark barrel of his pistol, he'd sworn to God he would shoot her, and she believed him. She had put her hands up and taken her place back on the cold, hard floor, and he had left her there, broken and alone.

She hadn't heard from him until now, when he'd come down those stairs transfixed not on her but the flowers, arranging them with careful fingers until she'd forced the question out of her mouth.

"What are you doing?"

He ignored her, staring at a brittle bunch of what looked

like poppies, lilies, and a piece of ivy tied together with frayed string. She noticed he had changed his clothes. The white T-shirt was gray. His jeans were a darker denim.

"Hey!" She shouted it, feeling the rawness in her voice. "I'm talking to you, motherfucker."

He stopped. Turned to face her.

"What did you call me?"

"I want you to tell me what you're doing. I want to know why you're standing there playing with those stupid *fucking* flowers."

He smiled, crouching to meet her, and she saw, for the first time, violence in those eyes. The irises had darkened. The sockets were sunken. The bags under them held something sinister. Desperation and anger had provoked her to say something, but now she saw she had kicked the hornet's nest. Irritated the rash. This wasn't the same man she'd seen yesterday. This wasn't the Joseph she was familiar with.

The nervousness was gone. All she had to do was keep him talking. Keep him occupied until she could find a way out.

"That's what you think these are?"

"No." Debra struggled.

"Stupid fucking flowers?"

He nodded. Stood. Moved across the basement until he was under a bunch that looked older and less vibrant than the rest. He reached a hand up to meet it, brushing the lowest petal with the tip of his finger.

"All our lives, we're told feelings are fleeting. That a good thing can't last forever," he said, mouth open, neck twisted to get a better look. "These flowers are proof that that is a lie."

Debra was quiet. She watched him. Tried to make sense

of what he was saying and where she should place her next words.

"I don't understand."

He pointed to one of the flowers. "A smile." He moved his finger to the next. "A thank-you." Pointed to the next. "A look that lingered too long. Every one of these flowers is a moment. A preserved reminder of every time I *mattered*."

Debra stared at him. Saw his chest rising and falling at the stress the thoughts were eliciting in him. He meant it. He believed it. She could see that. His eyes were glazed and his arms shook. She saw a vein beating on the side of his head.

Debra analyzed him. She tried to see whether this strange man who'd dragged her here and tied her up filled her with wonder or dread. There was humanity there. Something real. But there was also madness. An unpredictability she didn't think was tame. She closed her eyes. Tried to swallow the nervousness gathering around her neck.

"So to you, these might be just dried-out flowers," he continued. "Stupid fucking flowers. But to me, these flowers are reminders of every time I felt alive."

She didn't know if it was what he'd said or the way he'd said it, but she knew, in that moment, she wanted to kill him. A warm, feral feeling rose in her gut that wanted to find the gun he'd pointed at her and take the light out of his eyes.

He stared at her like a preacher who'd just delivered a sermon, waiting on a reaction or response that would make him a god. He'd said words as if they had weight to them and all she did was hate him.

"What does that have to do with me? What does any of that have to do with me?"

Joseph smiled at her. Ate her up with a look not far from love.

"You're not the first person I asked to take a ride with me," he said. "But you were the first who said yes." Debra's back started to sweat. A cold heat pooled in her chest. She started pulling against the ties sitting against her raw wrists, ignoring the pain lancing through her broken fingers. "You were so pretty out in that forest."

"No."

"So vibrant in all that dark."

"What are you going to do to me?"

"I'm going to do what I do with all my flowers," he said. "I'm going to hang you up. Dry you out. Make the feeling live forever."

"Where's he going?"

Yanna heard the hurt in Seth's shout. Sensed the same desperation pool in the pit of her chest as they watched Joseph start to ascend the basement stairs.

"Where the fuck is he going?" Seth shouted again. "We have to stop him!"

Beside them, Debra started screaming, soaking the room with panic.

"I'm going to untie her," Seth said. He lunged toward Debra and Yanna grabbed him, pulling him back with so much force he fell on her.

"No!" Yanna shouted, her own voice fighting the volume of Debra's yells.

"What do you mean? We can help her!"

"They're memories, Seth. They're done. You can't change the past."

"But," he said, panting, crying, trying to free himself from Yanna's grip.

"Stop, Seth!"

She held fast. Grabbed his face. Forced him to focus on her. "Listen to me. Look at me. Think about what we saw when you shot him. If we want to find out what happened to Debra—what your mom saw—we have to leave it alone. We have to let it be."

Around them, the screaming continued. Movement caught their eye. She heard the sound of Joseph bringing something down.

Yanna saw the pain in Seth's face. When they turned to face Joseph, he was already halfway down the stairs. In his hand, he held a rope thicker than fingers and an industrial roll of tape.

When Debra saw him, her yells intensified, reaching a pitch that made Yanna's ears want to bleed.

In the moments that defined the rest of Yanna's life, she wondered what kind of person it made her, that she was able to watch the entire thing happen and not do a thing about it. That she stood there when Joseph used the tape to suppress the screams, when he tied the rope around her arms and legs, when he threw one end over a beam on the basement's ceiling and lifted her into a sea of flowers.

As Seth fell to his knees beside her, she wanted to look away. She wanted to close her eyes, but she didn't. Instead, she watched. Watched as Joseph held the rusted blade up to the light.

Watched as he dragged its length across Debra's throat.

17

SETH HADN'T SEEN the blood stain the cold, hard floor at Joseph's feet. After Debra's skin had started to sever, torn apart by the edge of the blade, the memory had vanished.

It had been almost three weeks since, but Seth had hardly seen Yanna. He knew that now, instead of indulging an addiction to Flood House, she had been spending her time searching the small town of Hunt, looking for an older version of Joseph Lethe.

She told him she didn't like the forest there. She said there was something about Hunt's trees that felt darker and denser, with leaves that always looked wet. She told him about the places she'd already looked for him. A bingo hall desperate for a lick of paint. A dive bar called Roseland. A motel called Waxwing Creek. She wondered whether Joseph Lethe frequented them, believing they would be good places to start looking.

As Seth took another sip of beer, looking out the window toward Stillwater's trees, he wondered when he would see another memory. Since they'd seen Debra die, and Seth had tried to stop a vision that was so traumatic and visceral it gave him nightmares, Flood House had been quiet. There had been no more sightings of Joseph, and no more sightings of flowers.

He was about to head to bed. About to finish his beer and turn out the lights, when he saw something out in the dark. A heavy mass of shadows gathered at the fringes of the yard, where overgrown grass met heavy trunks. He thought back to the night his mom died, where he had seen a similar mass of shadows out in the trees.

Seth grumbled to himself, wondering if it was another memory finally brought to life. He thought about how Yanna had pulled him back in the basement. The look on her face as she screamed at him to let it happen.

He grabbed the shotgun from where it rested in the kitchen's corner. She wasn't here to stop him. Not today.

"Hey!" he yelled as he stepped outside.

He saw the shadows react. He saw them shift in response to his yell.

He shouted again, confused, pushing through the yard's long grass. The memories shouldn't react like this. They shouldn't know he was there.

He tensed his muscles. Pulled the trigger. The shot ignited the dark, ringing out against the calm Stillwater air.

Seth inhaled as the shadow cried out. The voice was human, but he watched as it stumbled like an animal in pain.

"Wait!" As Seth approached, the man he'd shot had one hand clutched to his leg, the other out in front of him, shaking. "Please, don't shoot."

"Who the fuck are you? And what are you doing on my damn property?" Seth said, adrenaline shaking his voice. "Come on! Speak, goddammit."

The person panted. Seth could see he was old. He

could see thin, gray hair swept to the back of a wrinkled head. When he looked up, he should have noticed how patchy and unruly the beard was at the bottom of his face, but all he saw was the face of Joseph Lethe.

"Oh my God," Seth whispered. "You...you're real."

"Please," Joseph panted. "Don't shoot."

A fire ignited in Seth's stomach. A bitter bile of everything that had happened at Flood House clogged up his veins. He didn't know why the man who had haunted him was here bleeding in his yard, but in that moment, he didn't care. All he saw in his mind was his mother dying in his arms. The life slowly leaving her body. "You killed her," he said.

"I—"

"You killed her!" Seth screamed, pushing the barrel into Joseph's face.

Joseph lay on his back, panting. He rested long fingers on his chest. The fleshy wound on his leg shone in the moon's light.

"Did it tell you?" Joseph muttered, smiling.

"What?"

"The house," he said, nodding a lazy chin in its direction. "It told you, didn't it? It showed you what happened here."

"I..."

"I always wondered whether it would, or whether it was just me who could see them." He groaned, rearranging his leg with gritted teeth. "I used to come back. Before you and your mom moved in. A few times after too. It would let me watch them. The memories. I thought it would keep them safe."

"You son of a bitch," Seth said. By now, the anger had softened to sadness, and every word hurt to speak.

"Now." Joseph struggled, panting. "Now, I guess they're yours."

Seth didn't know what to say. He didn't know who to call or what to do with the man bleeding out in front of him. So, he did what his gut was telling him he should do.

He took one last look at the light that ignited Joseph's eyes, lifted the barrel, and pushed his finger against the trigger.

18

THE VIBRATION of Yanna's phone pulled her out of her slumber. She opened her eyes, taking a minute to confirm whether the brittle hum was real or another nightmare.

Her room was dark. No sunlight bled around the blinds or crept in from under the door. She looked over to her phone and saw the image of Gina's face.

"Gina?" Yanna's voice croaked with tiredness. She pulled a pillow from the other end of the bed, pushing it behind her head. "What's the matter? It's the middle of the night."

"Yanna, are you awake?"

"I am now. What's happened?"

"When did you last see Seth?"

"I don't know. A few days ago. Why? Is he alright?"

When Gina told her that Joseph Lethe had been shot at Flood House, and Seth hadn't just admitted to it but called the cops on himself, she didn't know how to feel.

The man she had been obsessing over was dead.

Seth had finished it.

It was done.

"Yanna. Are you listening to me?"

"Yeah, yeah. I'm listening."

"I said, I'm going to ask you this once and only once. *Did you have anything to do with this?*"

She thought of the weeks they had spent trying to call on Joseph. She thought of Marsha, Debra, and all the trauma they'd dragged out of Flood House. She thought of a man she had spent the last days trying to track down, navigating the seedy underbelly of Hunt for. And then she thought of Seth. A man she'd gone through her own trauma with. A man that she had made memories with, on the verge of dealing with a new, uncharted trauma of his own.

She knew he would protect her. She knew he wouldn't bring her into this.

"No," Yanna replied, voice firm. "I had nothing to do with it."

It had been five months since Yanna had moved into Flood House, but only now was it starting to feel like home.

She knew what Stillwater thought of her. She knew what the town said behind her back. She knew what Gina thought of her too, but to Yanna it didn't matter. None of it did. This was what she wanted. What she believed she was destined to do.

She took a sip of her beer, thinking of the times she'd seen Seth sitting in the same spot on the porch, doing the same, looking out into that dark. She raised the bottle to him, motioning across a yard she promised herself she'd cut.

She hadn't perfected the process. Not yet. But she would.

She already had a handful of things to draw the memories out—popcorn, dried-out flowers, and talk of Joseph Lethe—but it was a work in progress. A process that needed reworking and refining. For now, she would write down what worked and what didn't. She would document every attempt to coax memories of Joseph out of hiding until she got it right.

There were other methods she wanted to experiment with. Music, photographs, and books were all things she had tried in the last weeks to call new memories, and she intended to work on cigarettes and different meals next. There were still so many ways she could call on Joseph Lethe, just so she could kill him.

That's what she planned to do tonight, and what she planned to dedicate the next years of her life to. Helping Flood House with its trauma. A house that they had forced to face its past. If she did it enough, maybe she could rewire it. If she called and killed Joseph enough, perhaps the house could find peace.

Yanna pulled her sweater around her shoulders. She finished her beer and moved into the kitchen, pulling the door closed behind her. She shivered, putting the bottle on the clean countertop.

On the table sat a packet of popcorn and, next to that, a pistol with a bullet already in the chamber. She'd done this before, and she would do it again. Was prepared to do it as many times as it took for it all to go away.

She ripped the plastic wrapper off the popcorn, unfolded the corners of the bag, and put it in the microwave as she'd done with Seth all those months ago. She started the timer and the microwave whirred, assaulting the kernels with its waves.

It didn't take long for the scent to fill the room. The smell of butter consumed the kitchen, hallway, and basement, where new flowers were already hanging, drying themselves out.

She waited a minute. Two. She listened to the quiet and the way Flood House moved. Somewhere in its depths, she heard his voice. The low rumble of Joseph Lethe, a man pronounced dead.

Yanna exhaled. She picked up the gun and slid the safety off. In the hallway, she heard footsteps. The sound of a memory stirring. She thought of the satisfaction of seeing it erupt into flowers, and left the room to meet it.

ACKNOWLEDGMENTS

I rewrote *The Flowers at Flood House* three times before settling on the story you hold in your hands. Among other things, it was a story that helped me find peace with the idea that it can take a while to arrive at something that feels right.

I'd like to thank Shaina Read and Sean Thomas McDonnell, whose feedback was instrumental in shaping those rewrites, and Shawna Hampton for her sharp eye when editing the version that did feel right.

I also want to thank my partner, Joanna, family, friends, and anyone who's taken the time to read my work. You are the constant that keeps me going and your support never goes unnoticed.

ABOUT THE AUTHOR

J.J. Walker is a horror author who loves writing unsettling stories about small towns, old houses, and characters that examine what it means to be human. Originally from the UK, he currently calls Canada home.

Subscribe to his newsletter, After Dusk, to receive updates, free short horror stories, and more at jjwalkerwrites.com.

ALSO BY J.J. WALKER

BURIED BY SUNSET

WAXWING CREEK